1. This book may be kept three weeks. It is to be returned on / before the last date stamped below.
2. A fine of 25c will be charged for every week or part of week a book is overdue.

The author would like to thank the following people:
Sue and Edwin for allowing me the time and space to do my thing,
and for encouraging me to keep on doing it;
Brenda, Jude and Margot for their patience, enthusiasm and help.

Other books by James Pope,
available from Piccadilly Press:

DISHING THE DIRT
SPIN THE BOTTLE
WONDERS NEVER CEASE

SEMI-PERFECT

JAMES POPE

PICCADILLY PRESS • LONDON

First published in Great Britain in 2001
by Piccadilly Press Ltd.,
5 Castle Road, London NW1 8PR

A catalogue record for this book is available from
the British Library

ISBN: 1 85340 620 1 (trade paperback)

1 3 5 7 9 10 8 6 4 2

Printed and bound in Great Britain by Bookmarque Ltd.

Cover design by James Pope
Design by Judith Robertson
Set in 10/17pt Gill Sans

James Pope lives in Bournemouth, Dorset. He has worked as a
youth worker and social worker and is currently a lecturer at
Bournemouth University. This is his fourth book for Piccadilly Press.
You can visit his website at http://members.aol.com/topbookz

one

I'm here.

I'm still here, safe and sound. I didn't disappear into my black hole.

Louise said why don't I write this whole thing down so I'll never forget how it happened, and why it happened and how I got through it. She said it might help. So that's what I'm doing.

Since my little 'incident' I see her every week at the health centre. She has this tiny magnolia office on the first floor, and on the coffee table there's an arrangement of smooth pebbles and a very small parlour palm in a ceramic pot. We talk for an hour solid every time. She's lovely. She really understands me. She sits there and smiles, and laughs at my semi-jokes, and makes me feel like I've really got some good qualities, not just a load of bad ones, which is what I'd always assumed.

She says I seem a lot happier. Well I am! I've done my exams, and the summer's warming up nicely. Who wouldn't be feeling better? Well, me, that's who – because it's not long since I was not happy at all. I was in a very bad place.

But I'm in a better place now, and I'm not going back.

When I was six, my mother left home. I haven't seen her since. I don't really remember the last day I saw her, though I do remember the last day I *didn't* see her: it was two weeks after she'd walked out on me and my dad. She was supposed to be taking me swimming and she never turned up. Dad told me she must have had a good reason, but if she did I never got to hear it. I heard she moved away, got remarried and had more kids. Dad doesn't like to talk about her.

I don't call my mother 'Mum' any more. I used to, in my mind, even though she wasn't around. But after a while, when I never saw her again, and the birthday cards stopped coming, it didn't feel right, so I gave up.

I call Jackie 'Mum'. I used to call her Jackie, when Dad married her and I still hated her for taking my mother's place. But now I call her Mum, because if you think about it, she *is* my mum. Your mum is someone who is there when you need her and who cares about you, and Jackie does that. She deserves to be called Mum. My mother is still my mother, always will be, no matter what she did. But Jackie is Mum.

Everyone has good days and bad days, right? I think most people deal with the bad days – they shrug them off without a second thought, or have a sociable night out with their buddies and talk about their bad day until it doesn't seem as bad. They let the bad days fade and let the good days stay bright and clear in their minds. That's the healthy way to deal with bad days.

Some people aren't like that though. They can't handle the bad days, and it's like the good days aren't really good any more. They forget how to be happy. I was like that – I was one of those people who couldn't feel happy. But I *do* feel happier now, now I'm starting to work a few things out.

I'd always been a worrier, still am. Things bother me. I'm a perfectionist – Louise told me that. Even at junior school, if I made a mistake in my homework I'd have to write the whole thing out again: I couldn't bear a crossing out. Thank God for my computer!

Or if I fell out with Dad, it would take me ages to get over it, whereas he'd have forgotten it the next minute. And when Dad and Jackie first got together I was a no-go area for weeks.

I was always up for a laugh, but I could get really fed up about things, dead easily. If I had to describe me, I'd say I always had a serious streak. Things always went right down deep with me.

So, when I think about it, the day my mother left was my first seriously bad day, and it must have gone to the bottom of a deep, dark hole in my brain. It stayed down there, buried under more and more bad days that for some reason I never let go of. Without me knowing, I became one of those people who can't handle bad days.

I must have been collecting bad days, storing them away in my head, letting them mutate with each other until they had created a huge monster of accumulated misery, so dark and heavy that I simply couldn't carry it around with me any more. I was a dark, heavy raincloud waiting to burst, but I didn't know it.

Until something very odd happened.

two

It was a moment both lovely and sad. Sadness can be lovely sometimes.

I was sixteen and a bit, in my GCSE year, at a good school in a very nice town full of nice leafy streets and nice shiny cars. There were a few raggedy people in shop doorways at night, but it was the sort of town where raggedy people don't really exist, even though they do. That used to really upset me, the way raggedy people were ignored.

Anyway, it was a Saturday afternoon, early spring, in the town centre, all spacious and pedestrianised, with attempts at going continental here and there (tables and chairs on the pavement, and some sun-starved palm trees). I was walking along Church Road towards the bus stop, on my way home from buying myself some new acrylic paints. As I ambled along, a couple bustled out of Bond's Wine Bar, making me halt my stride for a second so I didn't walk straight into them. They were oblivious of me and everything else, maybe a bit sozzled after a lunch-time meal and a bottle of house red.

Normally you wouldn't take any notice, would you? But I was immediately fascinated by these two, especially the woman. She was all over this guy, arms round him, snuggling into his neck, kissing his cheek.

I knew this woman was in love. All her body movements told you that. The way she hung on him, the way she moulded her body into his as they walked. She adored him, you could see it a mile off. They walked along, entwined. I couldn't take my eyes off them and I began to follow.

The street was quite busy, but I kept back a bit so they wouldn't notice me. I walked straight past my bus stop – I had to watch. I sound dead dodgy here, I know, but I was hooked. They slowed down, and I could see them talking intensely. I don't think it was an argument, but there was some kind of problem. Then she threw her arms around his neck and kissed him, at first with her lips shut, but then they began to kiss properly. They were moving their lips against each other. A one hundred per cent snog! People were giving them sidelong looks as they passed, but they didn't care. They didn't care about the rest of the world.

But then, abruptly, in the middle of their kiss, the woman pulled away, touched the man's cheek with her hand and walked off, back up the road, towards me. I pretended to be looking in a shop window as she passed by. Then I turned and saw her take a left into Victoria Park. I followed her. She cut across the grass away from the main path, away from people, and I saw her sit on a bench under a big horse chestnut tree, and drop her head into her hands. She was crying, hard. She was devastated.

I wanted to go to her and ask her what was wrong. But how could I? She was a complete stranger to me. What would she have said if I'd gone up to her and announced I'd been following her and her bloke, and watched them snogging? So I turned back into town, caught my bus and sat on the top deck, staring out, thinking about this woman the whole way home, wondering why she kissed him so passionately and then left like that. Had she dumped him? But if so, why kiss him that way? My mind was whirling, trying to get inside hers, trying to understand her emotions.

Then I began to think about how beautiful she looked, and how weak and hopeless she was on the bench, crying. I knew she was hurting, somehow, whether she had chucked him or the other way round. I knew she'd lost something, something she desperately wanted. She was in pain. She was a sensitive woman, with deep emotions, a woman who could kiss a man like that, in front of the whole world – strong, yet so helpless. I seemed to totally identify with her: as I sat in that yellow bus, I felt for her, with her. I began to be incredibly sad.

And as the bus struggled up Richmond Hill, I began to cry, unable to stop myself. A woman sitting behind me touched my shoulder and asked if I was all right. I said yes thanks, and sniffed myself into some sort of composure again.

It was the weirdest thing. Where had all that sadness suddenly come from? I didn't know. I mean, I was just a geeky teenager with imminent-GCSE stress syndrome and a boyfriend called George. All the usual stuff. Mum had even said to me once when I was whining about school, 'You know what's wrong with you? Teenage blues.' I'd nodded sullenly and agreed, and gone up to my room and cursed at my plastic troll, then laughed and felt better. I was just a normal adolescent.

But, I was wondering, would something as insignificant as two strangers having a tiff turn a *normal* adolescent into a pile of baby food? I didn't know what was going on in my head – I didn't know it was the start of my depression. I didn't know a misery monster was about to run amok with my life.

three

When I got home, Mum was waiting for me in the kitchen. Immediate static.

'Belinda? Where have you *been?* You know Dad and I are entertaining tonight. I need you to get the dining-room ready. Had you forgotten you said you'd help?'

'No, I hadn't forgotten! It's only half-four. There's plenty of time yet.'

'I want everything to be ready. You *did* say you'd hoover the carpet and do the table.'

'Yeah, I know. I will.' I sat down at the strip of fake wood Dad lovingly called his 'breakfast bar'.

'Well, could you do it now?'

'OK! Give me a chance to get in. Can't I have a cup of tea first?'

'Of course, but don't hang around – I'm behind schedule.'

'OK, Mum.' Don't get the wrong end of the stick about Mum. She's not a wicked stepmother or anything like that – she's really nice and I love her. But she could be very tense.

I shut up because it was obvious we were going to have a row if I didn't. She always got hypered-out when they were having friends round, and it was always me who got it in the neck. Where was Dad? Why wasn't he in the kitchen, rushing around like a fart in a colander? I'll tell you where Dad was – playing golf.

I went into the dining-room and started to take cutlery out of the cupboard. The tablecloth was always clinically spotless, but Mum had put another one out, so I got rid of the 'dirty' one and spread the 'clean' one. I set the places – six. Tonight it was Gregory and his wife and Sherry and her new boyfriend, whose name I can never remember. (Sherry is Mum's best friend and she's nice, but she's got a tragic habit of always going out with utter spam-heads.)

I got the Hoover from under the stairs, plugged it in and switched it on. The carpet was absolutely immaculate, and if I had actually bothered to vacuum it, all I'd have been sucking up was carpet fibre. So I sat at the table and pushed the Hoover back and forth so it would sound like I was doing something. As long as there was convincing noise, Mum would carry on with her frantic food preparation and leave me alone.

I fell into a lovely, melancholic daydream about the woman on the street. I began to imagine her, so deeply in love that she didn't care who saw her kissing her man. She was so full of passion but she and her lover had decided to part, probably because she was dedicated to her career and he knew their love mustn't come between a woman and her mission in life. Beautiful, romantic, heroic, glamorous, straight out of Hollywood. It made me sad again, but I somehow liked it.

I snapped out of my reverie when Mum called to ask me if I could peel some potatoes when I'd finished hoovering. I was a bit annoyed, because she'd broken my little spell.

I spotted one of Mum's gold earrings on the carpet, half-hidden under the sideboard. The other one was still on the drinks cabinet where Mum had left it, probably at the last dinner party. She always took her earrings out when she'd had a few drinks and she must have dropped this one without noticing. I studied it for a few seconds, and then I sucked it up into the Hoover. It rattled loudly as it made its way along the hose and I laughed, an unexpected, spiteful laugh. But it wasn't like me to be spiteful, not at all, and as soon as the laugh subsided I felt dreadful for finding it funny. For a second though it had made me feel better to do something nasty. It was a weird sensation.

As I sat there, sucking the last threads of the carpet into the Hoover, I began to wonder about myself. I was still feeling sad, but it didn't seem to be about the woman on the street any more – it seemed to be about everything. And it wasn't a delicious, romantic sadness any more – it was just gloomy. I'd been feeling less than on top of the world for a while lately, but I'd just ignored it. Today though, it was something a whole lot worse.

I walked into the kitchen, having tidied the Hoover away in its own special little storage space under the stairs. I didn't tell Mum about the earring – I felt ashamed of myself. Later that evening, Mum was looking for the lost earring and I had to sneak under the stairs and dig the earring out of the Hoover bag – I made out I'd found it stuck behind the sofa cushion. Mum was so grateful to me. I never told her the truth and I still feel bad about that.

'Do you want to join us tonight?' Mum asked. They always invited me, but I never wanted to spend the evening with their friends. My stepbrother, Sam, used to, before he left for uni, but Sam is good at all that social mixing and chit-chat stuff. It wasn't my scene. I said, 'No thanks. I expect I'll go out with Denise.'

That was a lie for a start – there was something else on my mind. I had this history essay to do, that I'd been putting off, and I was thinking about how bored I was by it, and I hadn't even started it. Half an hour later I had peeled the potatoes and the carrots and chopped up some onions, and I was feeling really cheesed off.

Then my mobile rang. I downed tools and disappeared into the lounge to answer it. It was Denise, my best friend. Loud, proud, don't-give-a-monkeys-what-you-think Denise.

We've been mates since we were eight, ever since we met at Saturday morning swimming lessons. What sealed our friendship was the time a kid called Adam spent the whole lesson taking the mickey out of Denise, because (to be fair to Adam) she swam like a brick without armbands. Anyway, we told the teacher we had to leave early and sneaked into the boys' changing-rooms while they were all still in the lesson. We found

Adam's clothes, ran them under the shower and hung them back on the hook, soaking wet. Oh God, we could barely breathe for laughing, but we got changed and scarpered. We waited in the car park and hid behind a tree – when he came out he was wearing all these squelching wet clothes, and his Mum went mad.

'Hi!' Denise bellowed into my ear. I could feel my eardrum throbbing in protest. 'Where are we going tonight?' If ever Denise starts a conversation differently, I will pass out there and then. Luckily she never did, and never has.

'Uh, I don't think I'm coming out,' I replied.

'WHAT?! We always go out on Saturday. It's the law.'

'Well, don't throw a wobbly. I just don't feel like it. I'm really behind with that essay for Slob.'

'Oh forget him! He won't even remember he set it, he's such a slob. Come on, Belle Of The Ball – what about meeting the boys in Jingles and then going to the flicks? Aren't you seeing George? . . . Belinda? Are you there?'

'Oh, Denise, don't. Look, I promise I'll come next week, but I really don't feel like it, all right? I've had Mum at me already because I came in late, and if I don't do my homework Dad'll moan.'

'Well, I don't see what that's got to do with you not coming out.'

'I just don't feel like being sociable.'

'But, it's Saturday. It's the day God created for going out.'

'How do you know?'

'Because, why do you think he took Sunday off?'

'Dunno.'

'He had a hangover!'

I laughed at my mad friend.

'Anyway, are you coming out?' she continued. 'We had a great time last week, didn't we? You nearly got off with that guy in the silver trainers. Bad move though, to chat him up while George was watching.'

'Don't talk about George. I think I've got a problem with George.'

'Oh, George is nice.'

'Yeah, nice, but still a semi-boy. He doesn't even know how to kiss.'

'*You* don't know how to kiss!'

'No, well, boys are supposed to know. That's how they talk anyway, like they know all that stuff. I think I'm losing interest in boys.'

'Right! I'm coming round now. You're beginning to worry me!'

'No, Denise, seriously. I'm staying in tonight. I don't really want to see anyone.'

'Not even your friend who loves you?'

'Well, not tonight.'

She gave up after that, and I went up to my room, feeling like a wet weekend, but also not able to do a thing about it. I didn't want to be sociable and jolly. I'd got myself into a mood where I didn't want to see anyone, or have to talk. I'd been getting like that a lot since I started my GCSEs. It felt like so much depended on me doing well. Dad was being really picky about my marks too, and checking my work and suggesting improvements. He would say he was just trying to encourage me to achieve my full potential, but it felt like I was never quite good enough for him. He was going on about how important these two years were, and how he wished he'd done better at school, and just look at Sam soaring off into the stratosphere at university, blah blah blah.

Sometimes I'd get annoyed and we'd have an argument, but then I'd feel terrible. I couldn't cope with arguments, but I seemed to be having them a lot, with George too.

I looked round my room, angry with something I couldn't name. I just wanted to destroy something. Don't know why, really. I grabbed my dress-making scissors, got hold of my plastic troll, and chopped his candy-floss hair off, right down to his plastic scalp. He looked back at me, so forlorn that I had to kiss him immediately to make up. It wasn't Troll's fault I was in a foul mood.

I put on a CD, some chainsaw-guitar band with psycho-vocals, and pumped the volume right up. I was goading myself into a really silly strop, and it wasn't making me feel any better at all.

four

I re-emerged a bit later and made some supper for myself, while Mum continued with her mission to cook enough food to feed the five thousand. Dad came back from his golf, beaming from a good afternoon on the greens (and the clubhouse afterwards). He came over to me and gave me a big sloppy kiss with his breath all cigar-smoky. I always liked his big-cuddly-bear kind of affection, but I was in the kind of mood where I didn't want to show it, so I winced.

'How's my precious?' he said.

'All right,' I replied, in that tone which means not all right.

'Good. I'm going to have a shower and get ready. Is dinner on the go?'

'Yes, it'll be ready. Cinderella's done her work, don't worry.'

'Oooh! Prickly! *Very* prickly! Did you get your paints?'

'Yes. I got this beautiful deep indigo. Do you want to see it?'

'Later, Lovely, all right? I'm a bit behind schedule.'

'Right.'

'Have you got homework?'

'Yes, and no I'm not going out, so I'll get it all done, don't worry.'

'I thought you were going out with Denise,' Mum chipped in.

'No, there's nothing going on,' I said. I didn't know why I was lying – I just didn't feel like communicating.

I went back up to my room. I could hear Dad and Mum talking in their bedroom. She was nagging him for being late and he was being all sweet and apologetic. That was their way, and they were happy.

I went into the bathroom, undressed and ran a bath. I lay in the bath, thinking about my mystery woman again. I had a lovely daydream about her and her boyfriend and their tragic separation. I knew she'd be back with him before long – perhaps true love has to endure pain before it can be called 'true'. That was how my brain used to meander.

After my bath I went into my room and lay on the bed in my pyjamas, just listening to Dad and Mum. They were arguing now, presumably about their impending dinner date with their friends, the TubbyBellies. I couldn't really hear what they were saying, but the tones of their voices began to make me angry again. I wanted to be in my mystery woman's world of well-made clothes and passionate encounters on the street, and romantic sacrifice that nevertheless left you a better person. Instead what I was getting was trivial noise pollution. I couldn't take it. I bashed the wall and shouted, 'I'm trying to study!'

They didn't hear me, or they ignored me. They kept on bickering.

My head began to throb, like it does when a giant headache's on its way. I felt so down, so totally cheesed off with everything. I knew I should have gone out with Denise. Jingles was only a coffee bar in town, but it could be fun, and the cinema was usually a laugh – we never paid much attention to the film. I certainly didn't want to do Slob's essay. I just felt like I couldn't be bothered to do anything at all. And I realised I did have a headache, right across the front of my head. I was miserable and frustrated. I wanted to shout, scream, do some damage to something or someone. Dad, Mum, any of their overfed friends, Slob . . . but they weren't available.

Then, I don't know why, I grabbed one of my graphic pens, the sort with very fine metal nibs, as sharp as needles, and I started to write on my forearm.

I wrote, 'Belinda' in black Indian ink, in bold ornate lettering, almost like a tattoo. It was strange, unfamiliar lettering, as if someone else had written it, not quiet, studious, middle-of-the-road me. When I'd finished, I noticed I was bleeding, just a bit, on the 'a' of my name. I must have been pressing too hard, but it hadn't hurt. That was odd.

I flopped back on my bed, breathing hard. I felt better. I couldn't have told you why I felt better, I just did. Now my arm hurt a bit, but I found it took my mind off the horrible feeling of my misery monster sloping around inside my head.

I thought about that woman again. I bet she had a tattoo, a sexy rose just above her hip, or a heart with her lover's name in it on her shoulder. I had this picture of her – dead prim and proper at work, but in reality a sex-bomb rebel who did whatever she wanted whenever she wanted, with whomever she wanted. That was how I wanted to be. That was how I was going to be. I decided to make a start at school on Monday.

five

Science was my nemesis, and if you don't know what that means, it means basically I was rubbish at it. Denise said I was good at it, but she was the sort of person who didn't mind a C. I wanted an A, and so far I'd just about been averaging B–. So science lessons were always a struggle for me: but today I had other things on my mind. I had George on my mind.

I'd decided that I needed to get a bit of spice back in our relationship because I knew I'd been a bit apathetic about 'us' recently and, despite George's inefficiencies in the lip department, he was nice – good-looking, not too clever, not too pushy. Plus, I had annoyed him by flirting with Silver Trainer Boy at the ice rink. I wanted to make it up to him. I had an idea. My mystery woman had shown me the way to go: I was going to be more like her and less like me.

It was just a normal lesson – Miss Frost came in, as she always did, two minutes late and had to spend the next ten minutes getting us quiet. It's the boys who make the noise really. They're like puppies – they can't sit still, they fidget. I think boys must have fleas or something, the way they scratch and pick their noses and play with their hair. George was the best of the bunch as far as maturity goes, and even he used to sit at the back of the class and flick rolled up paper at his mates. Sometimes I could get so hacked off with boys being stupid.

Still, George was worth some effort.

All through the lesson I watched him. Every time he turned to talk to Harry Chalmers, who sat behind him, I smiled at him. I'd read in a Sunday supplement somewhere that if a woman sits with her arms up behind her head, and runs her fingers through her hair, it sends a non-verbal message of sexiness and availability to a man. I didn't for one second assume George would know anything about that, but I did it anyway. If these things were innate, primal instincts, George would be sure to pick up the vibe.

A couple of times he kind of glanced sideways and smiled as he whispered to his pal. Another time, when I was really giving my tresses some serious sexy massage, he ignored me altogether. Loser! I was angry then. I couldn't understand how he could be so unresponsive. It didn't occur to me he might actually not like my sudden, out of character, public show of sexiness. I was so put out that my display of passion had been rejected, I just went temporarily nuts.

I was really out of control as I left the classroom. It was like my mind was jerking around at the end of a bungee, plunging and swooping between feelings. I didn't know I was going to do something extreme, and I'm still amazed at what I did.

'Hey, Belinda!' George was calling to me from the classroom as we all trooped out.

'Yeah?' I turned round and waited in the corridor for him to catch me up.

'What are you doing for lunch?' he said. Sometimes we would walk along the street and maybe buy a bag of chips, or sit in the woods beyond the school fields and chat or have a crafty snog. I liked snogging George, but he wasn't the most exciting kisser in the world. Sort of timid, with a little fluttery tongue like a humming-bird, that would dart back and forth as if nervous to be in someone else's mouth. I felt I wanted more determination in the tongue-contact department, but at least George was semi-sensitive and didn't just slobber all over you without a run-up. At least George would caress you a bit and stroke your hair before making his nervy dash for your lips.

'This,' I said.

'Uh? What?' George looked at me quizzically. I threw my arms around him and planted my lips tight against his. I pressed my tongue on to his lips and they parted, for a split second. But he pulled away. Everyone started laughing and some of the girls were clapping. George's face turned a deep shade of thundercloud-beetroot.

'You fool!' he gasped. He stood there, glaring at me in disbelief. The crowd fell silent.

Then he just turned his head, like he couldn't stand the sight of me. And so, like a total idiot, I dug myself in even further.

'You pathetic, spermless worm!' I yelled. 'You're as much fun as chickenpox!' Everyone in the corridor was staring to see what Barking Belinda was up to. For a moment there was no sound, no movement, just horror. I still feel like such a cow, just remembering the mortified look on George's face. He turned and stormed away up the corridor, with people now giggling.

'Do you think he's annoyed?' I asked the crowd. Without waiting for a reply I called after him, 'George! Don't go!'

He didn't stop and he didn't turn back. I suppose I could have chased him, but I knew I'd done a silly thing. I walked back to Denise.

'Wow!' Denise said. 'I've never seen you do something like that before. That was pretty exciting.'

'George didn't think so,' I said. The thing you must never do with a bloke, no matter how much you believe in equality between the sexes, is act the boss in public. And, overall, it's probably best not to cast serious doubt on a bloke's virility, out loud in front of his classmates . . . George's male ego had been punctured, and he wasn't about to turn around and admit to the world that he'd quite enjoyed being put in his place by a dominant female. So he just kept on walking into a lonely lunch-time, without me.

I was gutted.

six

I was all jokey and carefree in the afternoon. When I was with Denise I could laugh about anything.

'What do you call a man without a brain?' she asked me in a whisper as Mr Slob Rogers tried to explain to us the importance of yo-yos in the Second World War, or something like that.

'I don't know,' I whispered back, 'what *do* you call a man without a brain?'

'Normal.'

We giggled, and George looked round. 'Don't worry, we're not talking about you,' I mouthed silently. He didn't smile, he just looked.

'Hey, listen to this,' Denise was whispering again. 'What do you call a man *with* a brain?'

'Dunno.'

'A damn nuisance!'

'Please stop your whispering!' Mr Rogers commanded, folds of loose skin rippling around his triple chin.

We shut up after that. But it was a struggle: Denise and I

were such close friends we made each other laugh by telepathy.

I went home feeling quite jolly with myself. I'd shown the world what a woman could do if she felt like it. I'd been up-front and full of life. It wasn't my fault if George couldn't handle it. Why should *I* feel gutted? *He* was the one who'd lost out.

After dinner I was watching TV, being a bit of a slob myself, when Mum called in from the kitchen, 'What homework have you got?'

'Maths,' I called back. 'I'll do it in a bit. I'm watching telly.'

'Why don't you get the homework done first? It's a load of rubbish on TV anyway.'

'Don't worry – I'll do it!' I shouted back, slightly irritated that she'd disturbed my life-giving soap-time.

Then Dad came in and added his: 'Do you want some help with it?'

'Dad, don't take this the wrong way, but your maths is about as good as my nuclear physics.'

He laughed, but I think I'd annoyed him. 'Please yourself. But when are you going to get started?'

'It's all right,' I said. 'I'll go and do it now. I won't watch *any* TV *at all*.' Dad was only trying to be helpful. But it just used to get too much for me sometimes. I didn't need reminding I had work to do.

'Well, don't get stroppy. No one said you couldn't watch any TV – we're just saying school is more important, especially the next few months.'

It's not as if I didn't understand. I understood everything exactly. I knew what the next few months meant. They meant making sure you got a heap of good GCSEs; they meant doing as well as Sam, away at uni, with his ten GCSEs and three A levels, all great grades; they meant living up to expectations. That's what the next few months meant. I really understood that.

I switched the TV off and went up to my room. My troll was standing on the dressing-table, looking very pleased with himself in his red felt jodhpurs and his newly trimmed pink flat-top. I swung a high karate kick at him and blasted him into next week. He didn't seem to mind. Good dear Troll – still smiling, never nagging.

I tried to do my maths, but I was struggling again. I'm a pretty bright person, I know that, but nothing exactly comes easily to me. My grades so far that year had all been mostly B's and B+'s, with A's for English and art. I knew Dad and Mum thought I could do better – Dad especially. He had this way of saying he was pleased with my progress, which let me know he wasn't satisfied. I know they only wanted me to do well for myself. They did the same with Sam, and look where he was. I could see their point.

But the truth was, it wasn't only them that wanted me to do better – I wanted it too. I had this idea of perfection. Straight A's. I felt like I wouldn't be satisfied with anything less. But it was an enormous effort – I was already working at my limit.

I spent an hour on maths, and the numbers were swimming

in front of my eyes. Why couldn't I get my head round maths? I started to panic then, and I could feel my stomach tightening as none of the problems were coming out right. I had a revision book I'd bought, and I had the answers to check, and even with the answers in front of me I couldn't work the stupid, miserable problems out.

Then my mobile rang and started vibrating itself across my desk. For a second I was annoyed to be interrupted, thinking it might be Denise trying to get me to go out. But then I saw in the display who it was.

George! Gorgeous George! He'd come to his senses! He wanted to thank me for my public show of passion! I'd turned him on and he had to tell me!

'Hi.' His voice didn't exactly have the tone of someone who couldn't wait another second to hold me in his arms and kiss me until I begged him to stop. 'I wanted to talk to you after school, but you and Denise were busy laughing at some joke.'

'Oh, you know Denise – she's always trying to crack me up. The joke wasn't about you anyway. You should have come over. I wanted to talk to you actually. Listen, I'm really sorry about how I acted.'

'Well that's what I wanted to talk about.'

'Are you still angry?'

'Well, a bit. I was embarrassed.'

'You shouldn't be embarrassed if a girl shows you how she feels.'

'No, I know. But in front of everyone else? It's supposed to be private, that kind of thing. And you did slag me off, didn't you?'

'Oh George. I'm sorry. Shall I come round later and make up?'

'No, not tonight. Anyway, what I wanted to say was . . . I want to try a cooling off period.'

'A *what*?' I couldn't believe it. Not that he wanted to dump me – I wasn't surprised at that. But I couldn't believe he'd said 'cooling off period'! It sounded like a phrase from a car maintenance manual.

'Cooling off period. I think we should ease off for a while and see if we're still serious about each other.'

'Well why don't you just say you're dumping me?'

'I'm not. I'm just saying we've been a bit, like, tense, or something. Lately. You know. I'm not sure how I feel.'

'Well, I am. I don't think I do "cooling off periods". George, listen, I really like you and I wanted to show it, but if you can't handle someone with real feelings, then it's probably best if we stop seeing each other altogether.'

'Belinda, don't get angry.'

'Too late! I already am.' I hung up on him. Poor George. It wasn't his fault. I think he was only trying to be mature. He just walked into Hurricane Belinda at the wrong time.

I lobbed my phone on to my bed. Then I slumped. George had chucked me. I was numb. I'd been blazing angry only a minute earlier, shouting at him down the phone. But now I was just lifeless, a piece of meat. I went and sat on the bed, all hunched up with my legs pulled into my chest, staring at the wall, but not seeing anything. I should have been wailing my eyes out, but I just sat there, stupefied. It was like I'd been put on stand-by.

I wish now that I'd cried over George – you're meant to have at least a little weep when a boy dumps you. But instead I kept it all bottled up. I should have rung Denise and we'd have sorted George out all right. We'd always been like that with each other: when she broke up with Raymond Walmsley in Year Ten, I took her out to Piggy Pizza and we had two 25-inch deep-pan double-topping pizzas and then the Pig All You Want dessert. We were nearly sick on the bus home, but Raymond had ceased to be a problem.

I should have rung Denise right away, but I didn't – I stayed in my room, on my own, sliding into the hole where all my bad days went. That big old misery monster had just doubled in size again.

And then I got a weird flashback. While I was still curled up on the bed, I saw my mother, my real mother, as she used to be in my imagination: young, pretty, lovely, but also cruel. Why had George dumping me brought my mother out from under her stone? It was like any kind of sadness would set off all the other kinds in me.

I felt myself slip further into the hole, the deep hidden hole where my monster lived, feasting on my bad days. It's a horrible feeling. It's deeper than just being upset or sad. It's like your whole personality has been drained of light. I stayed there, hunched up for ages, in my room, in my hole. I did cry eventually, but I don't think I was crying over George.

I finally pulled myself up and went to my desk. There was always the homework, so I wiped my eyes and blew my nose and launched myself into that. I spent the rest of the evening making up problems to solve. I certainly knew how to hurt myself! I must have thought I could conquer my emotions by conquering maths! Mad or what?

I worked in fits and starts until eleven o'clock. I hadn't enjoyed myself, but I hadn't thought about George, much. I went to the bathroom and did the usual stuff. Dad and Mum had gone out and weren't back yet. The house was quiet and empty. You could hear emptiness in our house. When Sam had still been living at home, he'd have his music on loud. If Dad was in he'd be noisy all the time, just the heavy way he walked and shut doors loudly, and his deep voice. Mum would be talking to Dad or someone on the phone. Our house is big and high and very tidy, so when there are no people in it, it's hollow. You can hear hollowness; you can feel it.

I went into Dad's bedroom and looked out on to the street. A few people were walking along, on their way home from a pub, I suppose – young adults, well-dressed and laughing, the men hanging on to their women and the women laughing at their men. It looked fun. I wondered if they'd let me go with them, wherever they were going. Presumably they'd all passed their GCSEs and had jobs and places of their own. But they didn't notice me at the window gazing out at them.

I went back to my room and did some more maths. I remember folding my arms on the desk and laying my head on to my arms. I must have nodded off with my mouth open, because when I came to I found I'd dribbled all over my notepad and wrecked half a page of working out.

seven

I woke up next morning with George immediately in my thoughts. And then I was fed up, before the day had even begun. I wished the world had been blown up in the night and everything had been destroyed.

Unfortunately, everything seemed to be in its usual place. The world hadn't been destroyed, or if it had, some rat had come and rebuilt it overnight.

'Morning, Belinda. Sleep well? Want some coffee?' Mum said, as I drifted into the kitchen like a ghost. I think I muttered some kind of reply and she slid a mug of coffee across the breakfast bar.

'I hope we didn't wake you last night,' she said. 'Your father and I went to Roger's for a look at his new car, and we got talking, as you do, and then he offered us a drink, and it got late. Go and give your dad a shout, will you?'

Dad's got a lot of good qualities. But getting up wasn't/isn't one of them. He actually lost a job once for being late too often. Mum went totally up the wall about that, and she nags him all the time to be more reliable. I think my dad is a clever guy, but he seems to go a bit random every now and again. He once told me that he nearly cracked up when my mother left us, but that he kept himself in one piece for my sake. He told me he didn't really get over my mother until he met Jackie, and he'll be grateful to her forever for pulling him out of his rut.

Dad's got a pretty good job – he works for a design agency, doing all the art for posters and brochures and that kind of stuff. He's talented. He says that's where I got my artistic side from. I think I must have got my twitchy side from him too.

I gladly ran upstairs and bashed on his door, as loudly as I could. I always enjoyed winding Dad up. 'Dad! Wake up! You're going to be late for work!'

'Go away,' he replied, grumpily. I did the opposite and barged straight in. He was all snuggled up in the duvet, just his eyes and a mess of long semi-grey hair peeking out. I looked at him for a moment before I said anything else. As I looked at him, all sleepy and baby-cute in his bed, I really loved him.

I grabbed the end of the duvet and pulled the whole thing off him in one swift tug. He was naked. I laughed at his bare butt while he quickly yanked the quilt back and covered himself.

'Belinda! Go away!' he said. He pulled the duvet over his head and curled up again.

I walked downstairs, chuckling, and went back to my breakfast.

'Dad says he's not getting up,' I told Mum. She marched

upstairs and gave him an absolute tongue-lashing. In a trice he was shaved, dressed and gobbling down Swiss-style muesli like his life depended on it.

And maybe it did. Maybe that was why he wanted to live with Mum. She was no-nonsense, down-to-earth, and totally reliable. She got him to work every day, stopped him blowing all his money, kept him occupied with home improvement. That's probably exactly what he needed.

I sound like I'm criticising Mum, but if I am I shouldn't. She is Deputy Head of Personnel in a big insurance company in town, and she's worked very hard to climb the career ladder. She still puts in all kinds of hours, and she's taken exams to boost her qualifications. Her boss reckons she'll make it to Head of Personnel before long. And she will do it – she's just that hard-working type.

I ate in silence while they yapped, until I heard letters dropping through the front door. I went to fetch the post. 'From Sam!' I said happily, waving the letter postmarked Durham.

'Read it out, then,' Dad said. It was a little ritual Dad and Mum had that all Sam's letters from uni should be read aloud, and I liked it too.

'*Dear everyone,*

'*Hope you are all fine and fit. Did Mum get those new curtains? Term is going well – I presented a seminar paper last week and the tutor said it was one of the best on the subject he'd ever heard, so that was pretty cool. Apart from that, nothing much has been happening, that's why I haven't written before. How's Belinda? Hope the old schoolwork is going OK. Keep it up! By the way, I got offered the chance of buying a car, from a bloke in our halls. Could you guys lend me some dosh? It's a Ford of some kind, but in good nick and he doesn't want that much for it. I could really do with a car. What do you think? I'll pay the money back by working in the summer holidays. Anyway, I don't know exactly how much he wants for it, so I'll ring you at the weekend and maybe we could talk about it.*

'*Take care, Sam*'

Dad said, 'We bought him a new computer last term, now he wants a car! Can you believe it?'

'Well, he *is* nineteen, and I certainly had a car when I was nineteen,' said Mum.

'Yes, but your family were well off.'

'Well, *we're* not exactly broke, are we? He only wants a loan, anyway.'

Dad started going on about how things were different when he was a student, and how he had to work in the holidays for everything he wanted, and Sam should wait. Mum said there was no point in paying for Sam's driving lessons (he'd passed his test first time) if he couldn't have his own car, and Sam was putting us all to shame with his success and should be supported. And that's when I got up, walked out of the room and slammed the door so hard the stripped-pine dresser shuddered and a plate fell off the rack and smashed on the rustic quarry-tiled floor.

'Belinda!' Dad yelled.

'What's the matter with her?' I heard Mum say.

I like Sam. He's about the size of a blue whale and just as laid-back. But he annoyed me. It was more than a bit of step-sibling rivalry – he made me feel useless, and that little bit in the letter about 'keep it up' was enough to make me see red. He didn't mean anything by it, of course. He was just Sam – confident (cocky), clever (creep), good-looking (cheesy), successful (jammy). That's enough to annoy anyone!

And I knew he'd get the car, without having to pay the money back. Then again, I'll probably get a car too, because my parents are generous like that.

So, when I think about it, who was I actually annoyed with? Sam? Mum? Dad? Or my mother for not being there to stick up for me like Mum always stood up for Sam?

I went to school in a right state.

eight

I did try my best to make a good day of it. I think I was pretty good at covering how I was actually feeling, and I was straight into assembly, laughing and joking with the girls. But when I saw George, I felt like biological waste. I hated myself for acting so ludicrously the day before, and all my show of jollity was echoing round my head like a bell in an empty room.

Then again, in fact, it was only semi-my fault what had happened with George, wasn't it? Because I definitely did all the right things, even if they were too passionate for George's semi-mature brain. And I hadn't given up on him, even if he'd bottled it with me. He should have been feeling as bad as me, by rights.

Anyway, I'd decided to try my best to make it up with him. I don't know if I really loved him. I think I did. Whatever, I wanted to be the one who made the decision. If we really were going to break up, I wanted to be in charge of it. (Fat chance!)

I had a glimmer of hope at the start of the first class. He smiled at me as I walked through the classroom door, and I smiled back. I hesitated and didn't say anything, the teacher came in, and the opportunity had passed. When the lesson ended, he left the room pretty quickly, but I made sure I caught up with him in the corridor. It wasn't exactly private with kids bumping and pushing their way to the next class, but I had to speak to him.

'Hiya,' I said. I knew I was looking good. My hair had gone just the way I liked it, and I had on a new pair of shoes and my best blouse. I mean, any school blouse leaves a bit to be desired in the sex-kitten department, but this one was actually quite nice. I somehow had managed to convince myself I could pull off a *coup de coeur* with George, so I went at it with full feminine guile.

'I'm sorry about everything I did or said yesterday,' I said. 'I know what I did was really mad, and I'm sorry I snapped at you on the phone. I really don't want to stop going out with you. Would you give us another chance? Because, you know, you really mean a lot to me.' I know it sounds a bit shameless now, but at the time I felt it was the right approach.

'I'm sorry too,' he said. I gasped inwardly. He was hooked! 'I was, like, really confused.'

'So, no more cooling off period?'

'Well, I don't think . . .' He paused, and for a wild, ridiculous second of optimism I thought I'd won him back! 'I don't think cooling off is a good idea . . . I agree with what you said last night – it'd be better if we stopped going out altogether.'

I died. I swear my heart stopped beating. Technically dead. Flatline. 'Oh,' was all I could muster.

'It's just, you know, you have been a bit different lately, a bit odd or something. I don't feel the same any more. I still like you, but as a friend.'

How original, I thought. I wanted to get angry again, at how boring his thought patterns were, but I was jelly by now, and everything he was saying was actually perfectly reasonable. 'OK,' I said, 'I understand.'

I turned and walked away. I took a few steps and then I fell apart. Tears were just rolling down my cheeks. I was suddenly suffocated by this feeling of hopelessness.

I rushed into the girls' loos and locked myself in a cubicle. And there I sat, crying, until I heard the door swing open. Someone was coming into the room, so I made myself stop.

'Belinda?' It was Denise. 'I saw you running off. I followed you,' she said.

'Go away, Denise,' I said.

'I want to talk to you.'

'I don't want to talk,' I said.

'OK. I'll wait until you do.'

'Denise! Will you just get off my back?' I snapped.

'No, I won't, because you're my best friend and you've been acting really weird lately, and I want you to tell me what just happened with George.'

'Nothing's happened, and even if it has I don't care.'

'Oh, so why did we talk about him all the way to school this morning and why are you locked in the bog, crying?'

'I'm not crying!'

'Prove it. Let me in there, so I can see your eyes.'

So I let her in, and she squeezed next to me on the toilet seat. I told her what had happened. 'I am such a loser,' I said.

'No you're not! It's George who's the loser.' She hugged me and said, 'You and me need to go on a girly night out and forget all about schoolboys. They're all silly little tadpoles. Why don't we go down town and try to get in a club? The bouncers don't check your age if you doll yourself up.'

'I don't know . . . it's not my thing, is it, clubbing?'

'It'd be great!'

'I had enough trouble getting Dad to let me go to that under-eighteen club night at the town hall, if you remember. And it wasn't much good, was it?'

'No, because everyone was under eighteen! People like you and me need grown-up entertainment. We're *expected* to get in under-age. We have to at least try. It's our duty as teenagers. Come on!'

'I'll have to lie to Dad, then. He'd go savage if he found out I'd been in a club.'

'Are you in, then?'

'I don't know . . . yeah, OK.'

'Right, let's get to class. We're going to be late.'

'No, I'm definitely not going back. I'm going home.'

'You can't skive!'

'Well I am.'

'You never skive!'

'I can't face them all. They'll all be talking about me. George'll be laughing.'

'If he is, he dies.'

'No, Denise, I can't go back in there.' I began to cry again.

'Oh, Belinda,' Denise said, hugging me even tighter. We stayed there until I stopped crying, and then we sneaked out of the loo, through the school back entrance, ran across the playing field, and went to Denise's house. My first time as a truant. Another bad day for my monster to feed on.

nine

Nothing much else happened that week. But the weekend I remember, because I spent the whole weekend on my own.

Friday evening Denise rang to ask if I wanted to do this club thing we'd talked about. I turned her down. I really wanted to go out, meet blokes, have under-age drinks, be glamorous, come home late. Half of my brain wanted to let my hair down and turn myself into someone who knows how to have a good time.

But the other half had to stay in, see no one, get on with my homework, keep pushing, get the A's. And that's the half that was winning every argument. Now I'd lost George, I couldn't see the point of going out anyway: blokes were only going to be a waste of time. I'd tried being a strong, passionate heroine and I'd failed miserably. I just needed to work.

So Denise rang and I fobbed her off with a weedy excuse about tidying my room. I think she knew I was lying. She said, 'Well, I'm going. If you change your mind meet me and the girls at St Alban's church bus stop at eight.'

I made myself some supper and went up to my room. I

switched on my computer and started to look at my geography essay. I could write pretty decent essays and I could draw good maps. I could do them by hand or on the computer. I was good at that. Maybe that's what I'll do when I leave school, be a graphic designer like Dad.

Anyway, I started to read my geography book, and it was as boring as cricket. I wasn't interested. I couldn't make myself concentrate, though I seriously tried. I so wanted to be interested, but I couldn't be bothered. I wasn't tired exactly, just de-energised.

I logged on to the Internet and began to wander around the cyber universe, looking for nothing in particular. I put in a search under 'teenagers', just to see what it would find. I saw a link to a site called Teen Talk, so I went there. And I spent the whole of the rest of the night there. It was a kind of virtual Agony Aunt. You could e-mail messages about how you were feeling, and the site was jammed with all this amazing stuff.

I printed out some of the messages because these kids were so like me. So many kids with the same feelings as me!

Shaz@xnet.com

i feel like nobody cares or understands. do u?
my parents are really busy and expect me to put
in the same kind of hours they do. i work really
hard. my grades are ok. i am doing GREAT, i
think, but they don't seem to notice. i feel

like i could give up and they still wouldn't
notice. i feel guilty and stupid and sometimes
i couldn't care less. i am one of the best
students in my school and i still get yelled
at if i watch tv. anybody got the same trouble
out there? e-mail me.

Helen@freemail.net

My mother passed away nearly five years ago when
I was 10 and I still think about her 24/7. Some
days I feel so depressed I want to just not wake
up in the morning. Other days I feel OK. My
boyfriend is really nice but he doesn't understand me when I'm down. He thinks I'm unhappy
with him which isn't true - I really love him
and I don't want to lose him. The worst thing
is my father now has a new girlfriend and I
can't get to like her. I would like to know
how to stop being so miserable.

Jaz2457@netline.com

My parents won't let me live my own life. They
say I'm only 14 so I can't decide for myself
yet. I have to be home straight after school,
unless I have my music lesson. They don't let me
go to the youth club on Friday night because

there was some trouble with some older boys and now they say I should stay away. All I'm allowed to do is go to friends' houses. I feel trapped and if I don't go out I'm soon going to lose all my friends. Can you suggest a way to deal with parents like mine? My parents try to justify it by saying other parents don't care about their kids, but I feel like my parents don't care about me.

(This next one was the saddest – he's American, I think.)

Luis

I can't give you my e-mail address so you can't mail me back. My father reads all my messages and checks on my log-on time. He is so strict it's untrue. He thinks I'm downloading porn. My mom lives on the other side of the state so I don't get to see her much. I'm not a trouble kid but recently I got trashed a few times by my physics teacher because I was talking in class. He even mentioned it to my father at parents' night and I got yelled at for 30 minutes straight. My grades aren't so good. I was doing pretty good but now I'm probably going to fail a whole lot of stuff. I want to write games, but my father says it's a crazy idea. He wants me to study medicine like he did, but no way can I do that. He can't understand another person's view. Which is why I guess my mom left him. I can't talk to Mom, and my friends don't know I feel so low. My mom just says do your own thing, but she doesn't see how crazy my dad gets these days. I think he's still angry with my mom for leaving, but that's not my fault, right? I just want to do well for my dad, but he's never satisfied. Sometimes I feel like I want to die, like there's no point living because no matter what I do it won't be good enough for him.

I read pages and pages of it. Why do kids get so messed up so young? At first I felt less lonely, knowing there were all these other teenagers with the same kind of feelings as me. I wrote a message to that website, but I didn't send it. It looked a bit wet when I read it. My problems were so trivial I couldn't send them to the web where anyone could read them and go, 'So what?' Then I began to think I was such a pathetic person. Some of these kids on the web had *really* serious problems: all I had was a lovely home, a fantastically great friend, a father who just wanted me to do well, a stepmother who was trying her best to be a good parent to me, a stepbrother who was intelligent and cool, and an overactive sensitivity gland. If I compared myself to other people, it was obvious it was me who was the problem. Sam, who had after all been through a family break-up and ended up living with me and Dad, was doing fine. Denise, who had just as much homework as me, was doing fine.

I began to believe it was me who was wrong. I couldn't blame anyone else for how I felt, because I was the problem. That was the worst thing of all.

I was in this whirlpool of unhappiness – the more miserable I got the weirder my behaviour grew and the more I disliked myself; the more I disliked myself the more miserable I got. If I'd known where this was all leading I'd have asked for help. But I didn't know. My misery monster was taking over.

ten

For no obvious reason, after that night on the web, I had a few good days. I wrote up the geography assignment and my teacher was pleased with my work – maybe that was the reason. You can't always put your finger on it, but I know I had a spell of feeling not bad at all.

On Saturday I went out with Denise and our other girl-friends: we had a great night at a Mexican restaurant at the QuaySide – we ordered *everything* off the sweet menu, to the utter delight of all the other punters. The waiter had to come to our table about twenty times before we had all our puddings! We behaved like film stars all evening.

I began to imagine that I could handle things after all. I could study, and have a social life, and it certainly wasn't a calamity that George had thrown away his chance for fulfilment in love. As Denise pointed out, any bloke who'd let *me* get away wasn't worth worrying about. Troll gave me more pleasure than George had ever done. True, I hadn't had the courage to speak to George since our (throat-clearing cough) 'separation', but I thought I'd dealt with the situation. And when I saw him walking up the corridor at school with Charlotte Townsend, looking so slimy-slug-smug, I felt I was well and truly over him. That was a relief. One less thing to stress out about.

So things were all right, for a bit.

But the snag with me was that I could find stress anywhere, anytime, without even looking. And just after half-term, when I'd had a pretty calm week off, and Sam had visited and it had been a laugh to have him around showing off his 'new', bashed-up Ford (Mum had shelled out, as I predicted), I dropped myself back in my misery hole again.

I remember walking home from school on Friday feeling good about myself, because me and Denise, and a couple of the other girls we hung around with, had spent the afternoon huddled at the back of the art studio telling each other funny stories and doodling satirical sketches of boys' anatomies, hidden under our still-life drawings. Academically not very productive, I'll admit, but the sort of afternoon that sometimes feels great. Just being a teenager and being funny, and knowing the teacher can't enter your special little world, is enough to make you feel invulnerable, in with the in-crowd, exclusive.

I'd been invited to a 'soirée' at Erin Randall's on Saturday and Denise and I had been planning our outfits. I was nearly whistling as I stepped into the house, into the kitchen. Mum was already home, sitting at the breakfast bar, smoking and drinking coffee.

'Hiya,' I said, all breezy and light.

'Hi. Had a good day?'

'Yeah, same as usual, you know,' I said.

'That's good,' said Mum.

'You're home early,' I remarked, still feeling pleased with myself.

'Yes. I've had the afternoon off so I could do a bit of shopping for the dinner party. It's so busy at Insanesbury's on Fridays. It's a nightmare – you can hardly park down there. It's chaos.' She started off on one of her soliloquies about the problems of modern-day superstore shopping, and I laughed at her while I sipped coffee.

Dad came home, singing cheesy pop songs as was his wont, and we all sat together, chatting about nothing much. It was nice when we were like that. After dinner I went to my room, and started to think about my strategy for having fun the next day, and that's when things started to slip again. I found myself glancing at the maths books that were on my desk.

I'd intended not to do any homework that night – I was going to watch TV, maybe go to Denise's for a gossip and listen to CDs. But I stupidly opened the maths book and looked at some stuff I'd been trying to figure out. Stuff I hadn't really under-stood. And it didn't take long before I was panicking, realising I still couldn't really understand the equation or whatever I was supposed to be able to do. I could have left it until Monday and then asked the teacher, but no, I had to make myself do the work now. It was like a self-inflicted torture where I forced myself to do things I couldn't do, until I could do them, or until I fell asleep at my desk. Like Buffy the Vampire Slayer doesn't want to be the Slayer, but she knows she has to carry on for the good of humanity, I didn't want to be a perfect student, but I had to carry on for the good of . . . what? My parents? They wanted me to do my best work, but I'm sure they never meant for me to go loopy over it. Maybe I was doing it for myself, then: maybe I needed to prove something to me. Maybe I wanted to show my mother, in some irrational way that would never make sense, that I was better than the helpless little girl she'd dumped on ten years ago.

But, most of all, I think I was simply trying to be perfect. Because, if perfection were actually possible, I had to achieve it. Because, what if the only way to find true satisfaction was to get ten straight A's?

It was an obsession, I suppose. I talked myself into believing I would be happy if I just worked hard enough. I wanted to be Denise, but I was stuck with Belinda. I wanted not to worry about anything, but I worried so much I could never be content. I stayed in my room all evening until I fell asleep, fully dressed, on my bed, exhausted.

I'd twisted myself out of a good mood into a bad one. So stupid of me. And what I did at Erin's was even more stupid. Falling face first in a wet cow-pancake on live TV would have been more dignified.

eleven

I spent Saturday working on an English essay. I really wanted to get as much of that essay done as I could, so I wouldn't be feeling guilty about not having finished it. I worked through the morning and, as it turned out, most of the afternoon, writing and re-writing my essay. It went pretty well, and by the time I had to stop I was feeling a lot better, almost pleased with myself.

Erin Randall was a nice girl, and lucky enough to live in a massive house on the posh side of town, and therefore someone whose soirées were well worth attending.

I was dead excited by the time Denise's mum arrived to give us a lift to Erin's. I'd spent an age getting myself ready – Mum had agreed to let me borrow her black patent leather high heels, and I was wearing my slinkiest black party dress. I couldn't say, even after all the counselling, who the real me is, but this was a me I liked. 'Belle of the Ball', Denise used to call me when I was in party mode.

We looked fantastic as we walked arm-in-arm up Erin's drive

in our heels and best get-ups. 'I tell you what,' I said, 'any bloke who lands us tonight is going to have to be pretty damn special – we are hot!'

It turned out to be a bit more than a soirée too. Erin's house was more like a mansion with, it seemed like, an endless supply of rooms for dancing, eating, snogging, etc. There were loads more people there than Denise and I had been expecting, and plenty of new boys. Erin introduced us to some of her brother's mates, and we did a good job of introducing ourselves to anyone else who looked vaguely spot-free. We were choosy, as must be obvious.

Erin's parents had secreted themselves in a far off part of the house, and we young dudes had the run of the place. Technically, of course, there wasn't supposed to be any alcohol, but Erin's brother was eighteen and his pals had a stash that they seemed willing to share with us girlies. Denise and I had a fine time, dancing, pickling ourselves in a polite way, and sampling party snacks we'd never heard of before, let alone eaten. I was happy, definitely. I can clearly remember the feeling of being free of my misery monster for big chunks of that evening.

I found this guy called David, a friend of Erin's brother, and we were getting on like two sausages in a frying pan, when my evening lurched into madness. George walked in, with Charlotte Townsend.

I'd thought I was over him. But seeing him with her, at a party, obviously going out together, was a blow I hadn't anticipated.

She looked lovely, which was part of the problem. She had shapes everywhere, and they were all in exactly the right proportion. He was fused on to her body in an almost obscene way, but it was a way I wished he'd tried with me. He'd never been that familiar with me! What did Charlotte have that I didn't have? I had shapes. Maybe not such voluptuous ones, but they were of the same category at least.

Oh God, I couldn't take my eyes off them. My new friend, David, lost interest once he realised he was speaking to the back of my head, and he wandered off. I didn't know what to do at all. I was just a complete wreck, suddenly and pathetically. Denise must have spotted me standing on my own, looking crazy, because she came over and said, 'Hey Belinda. Where'd that gorgeous man go?'

'I don't know. Look at George and Charlotte. He's in love with her, you can tell.'

'Yeah, probably. It won't last.'

'I miss him,' I said, and I could feel my eyes already on crying-alert.

'No, you said you were moving on. That guy you were with earlier looked much more interesting.'

'I don't want him. I want George!' I was in tears now, and Denise was hurrying me out of the room, into the hallway. The hallway was crammed, so we went into a big Victorian-style conservatory and sat on a bench under some sort of palm tree thing.

'Don't get upset about him. You didn't even like him that much,' Denise was saying.

'I *did* like him. I just messed it up by being stupid. If I'd been a bit more patient, we'd have been all right. I bet Charlotte doesn't snog him in public.'

'No, well, she's a wimp then.'

'I still love him,' I said.

'Well, I don't think you can have him tonight, so you'll have to enjoy yourself with someone else.'

And, boy, did I 'enjoy' myself! I couldn't cope with how I was feeling by then – I just didn't know how to deal with feeling so dramatically crushed, so I tried to make myself jolly by behaving as outrageously as I could. I cruised around from bloke to bloke to bloke, had smoochy dances with everyone who'd have me, even when heavy metal was on the CD, had a few more little tipples, and ended up snogging Brian Brain (made-up name for Brian Whitehall, a really clever kid in my class) who I could hardly bear to look at usually. He was actually very nice really, but not my type – he seemed to wear clothes that only your great-uncle would wear, and I could be amazingly shallow for someone so deep.

I was horribly aware of George and Charlotte dancing and hanging on to each other like Velcro, and I made sure I acted out my best flirting where he'd be sure to see me. I'd show him what he was missing.

I thought I was really having fun, until I went back to hunky

David and asked him for a dance. He was standing with a bunch of his cronies, including some girls, and when I approached, a whoop of bitchy laughter and derision went up from them. I was a bit flummoxed, in my slightly tipsy state, and I smiled and said, 'Ooh, how kind.' Then a female voice called out, 'Slapper!' and I was finished. I turned and ran. I hit the outside and the cold air smacked me in the face like a wet fish, and I suddenly felt very dizzy. The next thing I knew I was sprawled out on my bum in a very unladylike arrangement of bare legs and high heels, in the middle of Erin's drive.

By the time Denise found me, sort of curled up in a ball against the garden wall, I had cried so much I had no tears and an almighty headache.

'We're going home,' she said. 'I'll call Mum.'

Denise's mum dropped me off at home and I crept in as quietly as I could. But I dropped my keys on the polished wooden hall floor and in the silence they clanged like an alarm. In the dark I couldn't find them again so I switched on the light. The big hall clock said ten to two and something in my fuddled brain reminded me I'd been told to be home by midnight.

twelve

'**If you ever do this** again you will be grounded for a year!'

Dad was coming down the stairs with Mum following.

He just launched into it. At first I didn't register that Dad was yelling at me. I must have been quite sloshed really.

'Did you hear what I said?' he bellowed.

'Yes.' I was startled into dumbness. I remember standing there in stunned surprise, and suddenly feeling my party dress disappear and my shoes vanish, and my make-up dissolve, like Cinderella when she stayed too long at the ball. Except that at least Cinderella still had tattered clothes on – I was stark naked. I was standing there in front of Dad and Mum, completely bare, stripped right back to my fragile flesh. I could feel myself beginning to shake.

'Well, what have you got to say for yourself? You're nearly two hours late. We've been worried off our heads.'

'I'm sorry. I forgot the time,' I whimpered.

'That's not acceptable. We told you home by midnight and you agreed.'

'I had to wait for Denise's mum to give us a lift back.'

'You could have phoned.' He was livid. There was going to be no reasoning with him.

'I lost track of time, and by the time I realised it was late, Denise had already phoned her mum so I thought I might as well wait, rather than disturb you,' I tried.

'I'm not surprised you lost track of time, judging by the state you're in. You're obviously drunk.'

'No. I'm not.'

'Well, you're clearly not sober. You look awful too – your make-up's all over the place. What's been going on? Tell me the truth!'

'Russell!' Mum stopped him carrying on. I began to cry, just quietly as I stood there, completely done in.

'Well for God's sake, Jackie. Look at her. She looks like a tart.'

'Well . . .' Mum couldn't think of anything to say, I suppose, because then she started to blub as well. Mum is one of those people who gets emotional quite easily – you know, for example, if she watches a weepie on TV. It's funny that she burst into tears then though – I've never asked her about it, but I still wonder why she did that.

'What the hell is going on?' Dad said. I think he really didn't know. He didn't know what he'd just said, or why I was crying, or why his wife was crying. His tired and angry brain couldn't cope with whatever it was he'd started.

'Well, it's horrible to say she looks like a tart,' Jackie finally said. 'She's upset.'

'Well, it's ridiculous,' Dad said.

'What's ridiculous?' I said, through my sniffing.

'The way you girls do yourselves up. You look cheap, Belinda. I don't like it.'

Then I was angry. 'Well, you should see yourself!' I said. 'You're always trying to make yourself look younger than you are. You look a lot more cheap than I ever could. And you can't stop me dressing how I want, anyway.'

'You'll do as you're told while you're living in my house, and I won't have you getting drunk either.'

'Well how are you going to stop me?' I shouted. Then I ran, to my room, my refuge.

Mum came up after a bit of shouting from downstairs. She knocked on my door and I told her to go away, so she came straight in. I was glad – I needed her.

'He didn't mean it. He's all upset down there now,' she said.

'Well, he shouldn't say such things. I'm not a tart. I just dress how we all do. It's our fashion. He just wants to stop me having any fun.'

'But you are two hours late and you didn't phone, and you have obviously been crying before you got here. Do you want to talk about it?'

'Not really. It was just a boy I thought I liked.'

'Well, as I remember, boys are pretty significant when you're sixteen.'

'Not this one.' I should have talked. I should have told her all the stuff that was in my head, making me upset. It wasn't just George, it was school, home, everything. But I kept tight-lipped about the really important things.

'So, was the party any good? Was it worth staying out late for and getting a roasting?'

'Not really.'

'Belinda,' she said with a new tone in her voice, 'are you quite all right? I mean, is anything bothering you?'

'Like what?' I didn't mean to be short with her, but I couldn't seem to be nice, even though I knew she was trying to help.

'Well, you know, to do with boys . . .'

'If you mean sex, no.'

'Well, anything then? Dad's right, you do seem a bit slurry, and if you're saying you aren't drunk . . .'

'What do you mean? Do you think I'm doing drugs or something?' Why was I getting angry again? She was trying to be kind.

'No. I just mean, would you tell me or your father if you had a problem? Only, you have been a bit ratty lately. It's not like you.'

'I'm all right. I just want to be allowed to have a bit of fun now and again without getting into a huge row.'

'But you do all sorts of things that are fun.'

'Yeah? Like?'

'You go to Denise's. You go out with your friends, you go to the cinema, ice-skating . . .'

'When did I last go ice-skating? I haven't been for weeks.'

'But you *can* if you want to. We never stop you. Quite often you say you don't want to go out.'

'Of course I want to go out! But I've always got so much work to do.'

'But that's the same for everyone. You've got to do well at school or you won't succeed when you leave. In years to come you'll regret it if you don't work hard now.'

'But I'm sixteen. I can't think about years to come. I want fun now. I want my life to be fun all the time.'

'You can't. Life isn't like that.'

'Why not?'

She went quiet, really quiet, and just looked at me. I think that was maybe the first time we'd ever properly made contact. She put her arms round me, kissed my cheek, wiped the tear dribbles away. It was nice. 'I don't know, really. I don't know why it can't always be fun. It should be.'

'If he would come up and say sorry, it wouldn't be so bad, but I know he won't. And then tomorrow he'll behave like nothing happened. It'll be "Morning, Lovely!" and a peck on the cheek, as if we're the best of mates. He doesn't understand anything.'

She was looking a bit blank now, as if she'd run out of energy for this conversation. Too many tricky teenage concepts for her, maybe. She got up and said, 'I've got to go to bed. I'm bushed. Sleep well, Belinda. I love you.' I didn't reply.

She was doing her best, I know that. And when she wiped the tear off my face I felt as if she did truly care for me. But I had already begun to hide myself away in my dark hole, and my misery monster was beginning to like having me around.

thirteen

I think people like Denise must have a special chemical that makes them happy about everything – like when she got the lowest mark in the class, by miles, for her Wilfred Owen poetry essay, I remember how she just smiled at the teacher and said, 'Do you think I'll be allowed to remain in the country having shown such disdain for one of the nation's most revered poets?' What a fantastic thing to say! The whole class died. Even Mrs Hutton laughed. Maybe Denise was disappointed inside, but what a two-fingers to the world.

She just read the teacher's comments, wrote a better essay next time, got a better mark, and that was that. If only I could have been like that I'd have been fine. But some of us aren't built that way. Some of us can't roll with the punches.

I think things really took a turn after the party.

That party was good because I'd shown myself I could have a fun time. Even though I'd had my entrails surgically removed by my father's words, after that party I couldn't stop wanting to feel good. For a while at least, at Erin's I'd been as happy as a beetle in dung.

But that party was very bad too. I had really made a fool of myself. I realised the girl who called me a slapper had been right. I couldn't fool myself into thinking it was actually very cred to get sozzled and try to get off with every bloke in sight. I don't think my romantic heroine mystery woman would have been impressed with my self-control!

And of course, Dad had been right too, and that made me feel even worse. I felt bad because I'd annoyed him, bad because I'd acted like a real dim, and bad because everything seemed to be going wrong.

It was so confusing – I'd been feeling really good, and now the very same things that had been making me feel good were making me feel bad. It's not something I knew about at the time, but apparently this is not uncommon for people with misery monster trouble. Louise and I call it my Rollercoaster Effect.

You can feel so high you could kiss anyone, do anything, fly to the moon, party all night and day, never stop. Then you can be so suddenly down you feel as if you're in a deep, dark pit with a rock on top of you – you can't move, you don't want to speak, you don't want to see anyone because if you do you'll have to have things to say.

Sometimes you don't know a low is coming until you wake up in the morning. And if you're going to be in the pit, mornings are worst.

* * *

The morning after the party I felt like death warmed up.

I lay in bed for what seemed like only a few minutes, but I must have been dozing on and off, because when I finally looked at my little metallic-blue bedside clock, it was half past eleven. I never got up that late, normally.

I tried to move and my head fell off my shoulders and smashed into pieces on the floor. When I'd picked it all up again it still felt like it was made of cut glass, most of which glass was digging into my eyes. My eyes were the worst thing *ever*. They were hot and dry and appallingly sensitive to any kind of light. I shut them again and tried to figure out why someone had poured quick setting concrete all over my forehead. It took another quarter of an hour to pluck up the courage to stand up and look around my room.

I didn't want to be awake.

The phone rang downstairs, and no one answered it. Dad and Mum must have gone out, probably for a Greedy Feast at The Dog And Hedgehog. Why is everything called something so stupid? I don't make up these names, you know – the world really is that crummy.

I started to walk downstairs, not really making the appropriate effort to catch the caller. The answerphone kicked in, so I sat on the stairs and listened. It was Sam, talking with his lazy, comfy style. He was planning on coming home next weekend. Usually I'd have been excited to hear that he was coming; I would have grabbed the phone and talked to him. But I just let him leave his message. I didn't care. I wanted to see him, but not much. I sat there, semi-conscious, even after Sam had gone. I just sat on the stairs, wondering what I was doing.

Then the phone rang again. This time it was Denise, sounding like she'd just eaten a hand grenade, her voice was so loud.

'Why's your mobile switched off? I'm going into town to spend some money! Wanna come? Ring me back a.s.a.p. because I'm going soon. Luv ya!' I listened and smiled at my friend's mad happiness, but I didn't want to move. I didn't want to see her. I couldn't handle her energy today. I couldn't work out though, why hearing her made me smile, and then made me feel miserable.

So then I went to the bathroom and washed. I got back into bed naked because I couldn't be bothered to get dressed once I'd got undressed. I shut my eyes again, and the things I thought about don't make any sense, even now. I imagined the phone ringing and it was my mother, my real mother, and I ran to the phone to speak to her and as soon as I spoke she hung up. It wasn't a dream, because I was awake. I imagined it as I lay in bed. I started to cry.

I started to think about my failure with George, and about what a slag I'd been last night, and how much homework I had to do, and how I wished I could be like Denise, and how I'd give absolutely anything to get fantastic grades, and how I needed to work harder, and how I wanted to be so perfect for Dad and

Mum, but I'd gone and messed it up, and now they didn't even bother to say goodbye before they went out for one of their disgusting meals. It all raged around in my mind, and all I could do was cry and cry and cry.

fourteen

I don't exactly know how long I spent in bed that day, but it was long.

Sometime in the afternoon I got up again and got dressed. Dad and Mum hadn't come back, but that wasn't surprising. They used to go out for a spin in the car after their big pub lunches, and maybe call in on one of their friends. So I knew I wouldn't see anyone until early evening. I was glad about that, because I didn't want to see anyone.

I went downstairs and into the kitchen. On the worktop was a note from Dad – *Whatever time you read this, hope you slept well! We're out to lunch* (I knew that) *and a little drive in the New Forest. Didn't wake you* (I knew that too). *Back in time for supper – don't cook, we'll bring something. Love Dad xxx.* I screwed the note up and drop kicked it across the kitchen.

I did nothing all day. And when Dad and Mum came home about six, I stayed in my room. I only went down for a bit of their Chinese takeaway.

I sat at the kitchen table and hardly spoke. Mum smiled at me a few times. Dad smiled at me once and, having done his duty as a father, retired to the lounge to watch 'Beat Up Your Neighbour' on TV. Mum started to try to chat.

'So what have you been up to today?' she said.

'Nothing.'

'Well you must have done something.'

'No, nothing at all.' I wasn't in the mood for chatting. But she wasn't going to let it drop. You can't really blame someone if they try to be nice to you, but I didn't want anyone to be nice to me. It was easier if people were horrible, because at least then I could get angry. But Mum pressed on:

'What time did you get up? You looked completely out of it when we came up to say goodbye. We didn't want to wake you.'

'I wouldn't have minded,' I said. I wouldn't have minded if they'd woken me, told me we were all going out for lunch together and to hurry up and get my rear end out of bed. I would probably have told them I wouldn't be seen dead in The Dog And Hedgehog with my parents, but I wouldn't have minded if they'd asked.

'Oh well, we will next time. I must admit Dad did say he'd ask if you wanted to come, but I said no way, you wouldn't be seen dead having lunch in an old fogey's pub with us.'

There you are, you see. You see how it goes. I always got it wrong. I think I'm being all self-righteous and I find out I was just being a cow. I smiled at her, and she smiled back. It was a freeze-frame moment. Our eyes really made contact. She really did seem to be trying hard to be nice – extra hard. Perhaps she was feeling guilty about Dad going off at me last night. Whatever, she was trying to be kind.

After I'd smiled I looked down at the remains of my Chinese and scraped the last few bits of noodle into my mouth. I didn't say anything.

'Are you OK?' Mum asked. For quite a few seconds I was quiet. I was thinking about the question. I didn't actually know what to answer. Was I OK?

'Not really,' I said finally.

'What's the matter?'

'I don't know really. I just feel . . . fed up.'

'What about?'

'Don't know. Nothing in particular.'

'Is it about last night? Do you want me to talk to your father? You know he'll have forgotten all about it. He'll be thinking it's all over with and there's nothing else to say. But if you're still upset, I'll tell him.'

'It's not that, not really. It's kind of everything.'

'Everything? I don't understand.'

'No, I know.' That comment hurt to say, and I suppose it must have hurt to receive too.

'Belinda, if I've done something wrong, just tell me. You're not making sense.'

I looked at her and our eyes met again, but this time didn't

connect. I could feel myself beginning to well up, so instead of bursting into tears and maybe getting some sympathy (which is after all what I wanted), I just went, 'No, you haven't done anything wrong,' and walked out of the room and upstairs.

I sat on my bed and looked around the room. All nice girly colours, nice girly posters on the wall, girly curtains. I wanted to cry again, but I didn't. I went to my desk and looked at the pile of exercise books waiting for my attention. Maths, geography, history, English, science, RE . . . all potential grade A's. Perhaps the odd B? No, B's were only semi-perfect, and I wanted perfection.

I looked at my room again and back at my books waiting for me to plunge into work again. Get on with your studying, forget all this nonsense about having fun, I told myself. But I didn't *want* to do any work today, I truly didn't.

That's when I grabbed my long-armed dress-making scissors and went ever so slightly mad.

fifteen

Even now, thinking back, trying to make some kind of sense out of it all, I can't really understand it. I just looked around, and it was as if the whole damn room was laughing at me. Everything was so nice, so smug and so co-ordinated. All the furniture was shiny and matching, the pattern on the duvet cover and the pillows matched the pattern on the curtains, the carpet toned in elegantly with the wallpaper. The pop stars on my posters were all gorgeous, my clothes hanging on the rail were pressed and pristine, my exercise books were neatly arranged on my desk, my computer's screen saver was dancing away merrily across the screen. Everything in that room was perfect, like a glossy film set.

And then I caught a glimpse of myself in my full-length dressing mirror, and I suddenly didn't know who I was looking at. I looked into my own eyes, and it was like I was looking at someone else.

You know that film where this beautiful woman works as a nanny for a rich, successful couple, and she seems to be the ideal

nanny, but really she's devious, and all she wants to do is wreck their perfect home? I looked at my own reflection and I saw well-behaved, well-groomed, pretty little Belinda dissolve away, as if a disguise had been removed. Behind the Belinda mask I saw some wild, passionate, dangerous teenager, someone quite different, someone who didn't belong in that perfect bedroom at all. It was like I was that baddie pretending to be a goodie, and I'd found myself out.

It was the most brain-breaking sensation, seeing Belinda as a fake. It only lasted a split second really, because I threw a slipper at the tall mirror and it angled up on its hinge so I couldn't see myself any more.

But then I had this bizarre idea, and that's where the dress-making scissors came in. I didn't mean to go so crazy, but once I'd started I felt so good I couldn't stop. I think I got a bit too caught up in my film scene.

I started by snipping at my pillowcase. Just slowly, almost calmly, as if I were actually doing some dress-making. I nibbled away the frilly edging, until I'd cut off a big long strip of frilly material. I laughed. I liked it.

So then I trimmed the frill off the duvet cover too. That took quite a bit of doing, as you can imagine, because I had to cut it off all the way round, without cutting into the seam.

And then I cut roundish chunks out of the cover so you could see the white quilt through the holes. I quite liked the look of that too – sort of artistic.

Then I worked on my curtains, which had been annoying me for a long time. I cut nice straight strips out of them, right up the length of each curtain, until what was left was hanging down in fingers of material.

I stopped for a minute or two and had a look at my room again. I really liked it. It wasn't half so snooty now, and the alternative Belinda in the mirror would have felt a bit more at home.

But the walls were still way too bright.

So I mixed up some really wonderful deep purple acrylic paint and, with the widest brush I could find, I painted lovely shapes all across the walls. They were abstract shapes, just whatever seemed to flow into my brush. The purple paint and the orangey patterned wallpaper went together surprisingly well, I thought. I used up a whole tube of purple acrylic. I took that indigo I'd bought and painted some winding vines up through the shapes and all round my posters. And then I got some green and painted a tall tree on the white bedroom door. I made it all wavy and light, like a willow tree that lives near fresh water. That was lovely. It made me feel very relaxed.

My computer looked totally wrong now though. It was too smooth, too antiseptic. So I painted that in bright red acrylic. I did it in rough, lumpy sweeps of colour. It looked like a sculpture when I'd finished. Excellent.

I didn't do anything to my posters, even the pop stars who probably deserved a serious make-over. I still liked my pop stars. And I had one beautiful poster of a horse running across the Camargue in France, one of those magical white horses that run wild. I didn't touch that. I've still got that one on my bedroom wall, even now. One day, I'm going to own a horse and I'm never going to stop riding, out in the New Forest, whatever the weather, and me and the horse will be so free.

I wish I'd taken a photo of my room then. I thought it was wonderful. The sunlight from outside was sort of chopped as it shone through my stripped curtains, and the purple, blue and orange walls shimmered as the light wandered across the new decor. My tree-door seemed like the opening to a new land-scape, and my bed looked like a piece of installation art in the middle of a funky art gallery. I was pretty impressed by what I'd done. My heart was banging at my chest, and I was breathing hard, exhilarated.

After a while, I angled the tall mirror back so it was upright and showed into the room again, and I watched myself in it for a few seconds, or maybe minutes. I could see myself properly now. I'd made my room just how I wanted it to be, so now I fitted. I could bin the fake-Belinda mask: I didn't need to pretend to be someone I wasn't. Restored to her natural environment, the impostor had revealed her true identity and she was jolly happy to be herself again.

But I'd forgotten I was still the baddie in the story, and bad-dies always pay for their crimes.

sixteen

I couldn't really blame Dad for what he did when he found out about my room. Any parent would do the same, especially if they'd spent their hard-earned money on making your room as pretty as it could be and then you trashed said room for no reason other than you didn't feel right about it any more.

But, then again, I'm not sure I'd ever be that hard on my children, if I ever have any. I think I'd be kinder, more understanding. Because, whatever anybody does, there has to be a reason behind it, and if my daughter disintegrated her room, I'd have to ask myself why. I don't think Dad ever really worked out why I did it. But it's the *why* that's most important.

I can't blame anyone for what I did, but I had to stop being that artificial girl in the mirror, or the real girl was going to fade out of existence. But I don't think Dad ever really got that. I know it sounds totally dramatic to say I was losing myself, but I was. I had to hang on to myself somehow.

It took three or four days for Mum to discover my modifications.

She doesn't go in my room much, and Dad virtually never does. I think he's embarrassed about being in a girl's room. It's hard for men really. They don't understand us. They might be a bit scared of us actually. I think boys, and men, don't really feel too comfy with women, close up. They like ogling over their laddish glossy mags in the newsagent's on Saturday mornings, but to truly be close to a real woman is a bit too exposed for most blokes to handle, and they keep their distance. That's why they spend so much time playing football, watching football, talking about football, wearing football kits even when they're not playing. It keeps them safe amongst each other. They don't mind physical closeness, like being within one millimetre of your squidgy bits, but they don't want to get too near your psyche. That's my theory anyway. And Dad definitely didn't want to get too near to my psyche once he saw my new room . . .

When I read back what I'm writing, I know I can seem quite up, quite clever and flip: that's how I am when I'm on form. I quite like myself, now. But at the time I was deep in my hole, and my misery monster was growing by the minute. I'd had this fantastic rush of excitement, but then I regretted what I'd done and by the time Mum found the room, I'd already had several days of beating myself up over my idiotic behaviour.

The thing about being depressed is that when you're in it, right in it up to your eyeballs, you can't think you'll ever be different. You think you'll always be that sad. But you get these moments of happiness that make you think you've solved your problem. Then the happiness just clicks off and you're back in your hole again. And being happy for that short snap makes you feel even more desperate, because you know you couldn't hang on to it. You have to believe me when I say I feel better now, but then I felt like giving up.

Everything I did that I thought was going to be a laugh, or cool, or make me feel strong, ended up making me feel worse. And it was no one's fault but my own.

Mum found my room one morning when she had the day off work and decided to vacuum the house.

What must she have thought when she opened my door and saw my mind whirling around on the walls in orange, purple and indigo?

When I came home from school, she was sitting in her usual place at the breakfast bar, reading a magazine and drinking coffee. She looked up at me and didn't speak, which was very out of sync for Mum. She always liked to chat.

'Hi,' I said, extra bright, knowing something was up, and really I suppose, knowing that what was up was my room.

'Hello,' she replied. 'Hello', not 'Hi', or straight into a story about some molecule-thin celeb she'd been reading about in her magazine. Just 'Hello'.

I sat down at the table. 'Want a coffee?' I could see she had one already, but I couldn't think of anything else to say.

She just looked at me. I can remember her eyes so clearly. They were mournful.

I looked down at the polished, antiqued pine and saw my blurry reflection gawping back at me. I felt sick. I hated myself. Any pride I'd had at taking control of my room had long since dissolved. I looked up at her again and her eyes were still fixed on me, sad as hell.

'Will you please tell me what is wrong?' she said.

'What do you mean?'

'I've seen your room.'

Of course, I already knew that, but hearing her say it, like she'd been bereaved, hit me hard, somewhere between my brain and my stomach.

'Oh,' I said.

'Do you know what your father is going to say when he finds out?'

'Not really.'

'He's going to go completely mad.'

'Why?'

'Why?! Because you've destroyed your room. How do you think he's going to feel? He decorated it for you, and you've wrecked it. I don't understand this at all. I want to understand, Belinda, I really do, but I don't. We've all been teenagers, and we've all had our little troubles, but God, we don't smash our homes up . . .' She had begun to shout, but as her voice rose it also trailed off, and she sat there gazing past my face. She didn't often get angry, only with Dad if she thought he was being lazy. But she never really got angry with Sam or me.

'I'm sorry,' I said. I was. And that was the worst bit. I *was* so very sorry, but the damage had been done. I could not justify myself. I'd hurt my parents, just to please myself for a few minutes of fun.

Mum's voice was sort of shaking: 'You don't just destroy a whole room on a whim, and then say sorry as if nothing has happened,' she said.

'What else can I say? I wish I hadn't done it.'

'So why did you? It's so shocking. It looks dreadful in there, like a hooligan broke in and vandalised it.'

'I got angry . . . and I didn't know what else to do.'

'What were you so angry about that you had to do that?'

'I don't know . . .'

'You must know!'

'I thought I knew, but now I'm not quite so sure.'

'Oh Belinda, this is terrible. It's as if I've never known you, and suddenly you've appeared in front of me and I don't know what to do or say.' So right, and she couldn't possibly have known how right.

'I'm really sorry. I won't do anything like that again. I just had a bad day and I couldn't handle it. It was like I needed to escape.'

'Escape from what?'

'From me.'

The room went cold and silent. Even writing it makes me

shiver. It is a hard, hard thing to say about yourself, and Mum couldn't take it on board at first. I saw her face sort of quiver as I said it. I began to realise then how she did really love me. If she didn't love me, she couldn't feel as deeply about what I'd said. It wouldn't mean much to someone who didn't care. But she looked completely blasted. Her eyes went wet.

'You don't want to be you, is that what you're saying?'

'In a way. Not exactly. But sort of.' It's amazing how incapable of expressing myself I can be. Sometimes I can hardly string a sentence together. It's a teenager thing. We go all enigmatic on adults. It gives us power. But the funny thing was, I wanted to speak, because I could tell this was a speaking moment, and if I didn't do it now I might not get the chance again. Mum was open for it, and I needed to go with her.

'That's a riddle, Belinda. What do you mean?'

'I mean, I hated being Belinda and I wanted to be someone else so I took it out on my room.' That was very clear, I thought.

'What's wrong with being Belinda? And why couldn't you have asked Dad to redo the walls, or ask me to buy new curtains, or make some yourself?'

I very nearly said, 'I did make some myself,' but I stopped myself and said instead, 'Because you wouldn't have let me have it how I want it.'

'But . . . you can't just smash up anything you don't like. That's not how it works. You can't simply destroy things whenever you've had enough of them.'

'My mother did.'

'Oh, is this about your mother?'

'Not really.'

'Oh Belinda, I wish I knew what to do or say. I know you must be very unhappy but –'

'How do you know I'm unhappy?'

'Well, it's pretty obvious.'

'Well you're wrong. I'm perfectly happy, especially now I've got my room the way I want it.' She was right, but something got me annoyed and I had to defend myself. I wasn't unhappy, I was just taking control of my life. 'Why do you assume I'm unhappy just because I don't like the way Dad did my room? I just wanted to have something of my own so I could feel it was mine. Is that too hard to understand?'

'No.' She was quiet. 'It's what everyone wants. It's normal.'

'So . . . what's the problem?'

'The problem is, if you just walk over other people to get what you want – that's selfish; it causes pain.'

'The room wasn't really my choice anyway – it was what you and Dad wanted me to want. It's only ever all right if it's what you want. If I want it, it's wrong.'

'I don't think that's true, Belinda. But anyway, I know you didn't want to upset me or your dad, even if you did hate the way he did the room, so I still say I think you're unhappy. Or you wouldn't do something crazy like that. Do you think you need to see the doctor?'

'No! No way. What for?'

'Well, maybe you're not well . . .'

'I'm all right.' That's the big thing I know now. I wasn't all right. I was ill. I can say it now, but then I didn't even dare think it.

She looked at me again and smiled, but it was a dying smile, and I couldn't stand to see it. I got up and went to my room.

Mum must have told Dad what had happened as soon as he walked in, because voices suddenly cranked up a few thousand decibels and just as suddenly dropped down again. Then there was quite a long time when they were obviously talking about me. There were footsteps on the stairs. And then I started to pray.

seventeen

When he finally came up to my room with Mum following him, urging restraint, I was quaking. My little fantasy rebellion was over and now reality was on its way up the stairs.

It was mercifully short. He knocked on the door and I bid him enter. He entered, looked around and said, 'How could you do this?' He looked a bit greyer than normal, I thought. He is a good-looking bloke, my dad, and he's able to look young and with it when he wants to. Sometimes he goes a bit far on that front – he can overdo the trendy gear. But generally I think he's the sort of man I'd like to end up with when I'm forty-five. But that day he was looking old. He wasn't as wild as I'd been expecting, but in a way that was worse. He stood at the door and stared around the room. All my creativity seemed ugly to me then. My curtains, that had seemed so cutting-edge (get it?) and artistic a few days ago, just looked like insanity now. I felt dreadful.

'Do you really think this is the way to make a point?' he said.

'No.'

'So what is going on?'

'Nothing . . . I just wanted my room different.' I was as humble as I could be.

'Oh it's different, no worries there. I don't get it, Belinda – you have everything you want, and you go and do this. You've acted like a spoilt brat.'

And then I stopped being humble and started being sarcastic. 'That's because I *am* a spoilt brat. I have everything I want.'

'Don't be smart, Belinda. Maybe you haven't worked this out, but you've only got the things you've got because your mother and I work our butts off all week.'

'Don't do it on my account. I don't want anything from you.'

'Oh, so you don't want new clothes?'

'No. I'd rather go to Oxfam.'

'You don't want your computer?'

'No.'

'And how will you do your homework without it?'

'I won't do it.'

'And what sort of career do you think you'll have if you flop school?'

'I don't want a career. I'll beg.'

'This is a waste of time – you're talking like an idiot now.' He wasn't shouting, but he was still livid. 'Maybe you don't appreciate what we do for you, and maybe you don't care about school or your future, but we do care. Maybe everything you want will fall into your lap without you trying, but we have to work for every single penny. This room and everything in it cost hard-earned money. I tell you, Belinda, I want to support you, help you to get the best of everything, but –'

'Don't bother. I'm an idiot, like you said. I'm not worth the effort.'

He looked at me. 'How stupid of me to think you were.'

The silence that lingered on those words was awful. I felt my insides wither as I absorbed the pain I must have caused him.

He began to turn away and said, 'You're grounded for two weeks with no pocket money, and you pay for the room yourself. New curtains, new pillows and duvet, and the walls repapered. And you had better pray the paint comes off the computer.'

He walked out of the room. I was left with Mum sitting on the edge of my bed.

I was done in. I started crying, and Mum hugged me and said, 'You've got to let us in on whatever it is that's eating you. I know this is about something. Please let us help.'

I couldn't speak. I just sat next to Mum, staring blankly into nowhere. I should have done what Mum said – I should have talked to them, really talked, told them everything that was in my head. If I'd done that, the rest of this story might never have happened.

eighteen

The two weeks grounded went quickly. I was so down by now that I wouldn't have cared if Dad had tied me to my bed. In fact I preferred being forcibly banned from socialising: it saved me having to say no to Denise all the time. Dad redecorated my room, and I paid for the new bed linen. I was glad I was being punished – it was right.

Sam came home for his weekend, but he was out with his mates all the time, so I didn't really talk to him. He kept well clear of any controversy where domestic decor was concerned – he'd had the same posters in his room since he was fourteen, I swear.

School was a waste of time. I couldn't concentrate on anything. I just spent two weeks looking out the classroom window at the playing fields. Sometimes I watched boys playing football. Sometimes I tracked birds flying across the field. Sometimes I dreamed of my mother.

It's easier not having a mother. You can fantasise that she's beautiful, intelligent, caring, understanding, creative. No faults.

Silly idea.

I could have handled my problems if I'd just put them into context. But I couldn't put anything into context. Everything seemed massively important, so important that it was overwhelming. School, George, my absent mother, my parents. It was all important stuff, but all stuff you could handle if you were basically happy. But I was basically unhappy, and everything I worried about made me more unhappy, and I was sinking under the weight of all this unhappiness. My misery monster was having a field day with my emotions. I could feel myself sinking, but I didn't know what to do about it. If I'd told someone how I was feeling I would have got a different view on things. But all I had was my view on things, and it was dark.

I would walk to school without bothering to call in on Denise, and when she saw me she would go, 'Belinda! Why didn't you come round for me? I was waiting and waiting! Don't you love me any more?'

I couldn't say what I wanted to say, because it would have been too painful. It would have been true, but it would have been too hard for her. The truth was I didn't want to see her. I didn't want to see anyone.

I didn't even want to be awake. I actually fell asleep in history one afternoon, and when Slob spotted me he must have made some funny comment because I was woken by the noise of the rest of the class laughing at me. After the lesson Denise said she thought I was pretty cool – she said she wished she had the nerve to fall asleep in history. It wasn't anything to do with nerve – I was just so tired.

But I couldn't sleep at night. All day I was in a fog, but I would spend all evening in my room studying, and then when I tried to sleep I couldn't stop my mind churning. In the morning I would be a zombie. I was working harder than ever, but I was so out of kilter that I wasn't making any progress at all.

I bunked off school two days. I forged a note from Mum, and because I was such a model student, no one at school questioned the dodgy signature. Dad and Mum never knew what I was doing because they were always out of the house before me and back after me. I had breakfast with them, then went back to bed, and got into my school uniform before they came home from work.

My two weeks grounded passed and I was quite sad to have to go back to normal life again. So I didn't. I carried on not going out, not seeing anyone after school. Denise would ring and I would put her off. I just worked and worked. I didn't even care about my room any more. Dad commented one Saturday night that I ought to take some time off, go out and see my pals, but I said I was on a roll and couldn't stop. He said he was pleased it was going so well. So I was doing better, wasn't I? Dad was happy. I tricked him, didn't I?

It was coming up to the Easter holidays. GCSEs were only a few weeks off. My marks had been very good, considering the bizarre way I was existing. There was no reason to suppose I wasn't on my way to a stunningly successful summer, A levels and then university. Dad and Mum would be so pleased for me. Everything was perfect. Except for me – I had never been so unhappy in my life.

I knew I wasn't going to make it. It was strange to be working so hard, but feeling so hopeless. My heart would leap with fear every time I thought about the exams.

Then, one evening, trying to keep my eyes focused on the page, my concentration just totally went. I desperately wanted to go out. It was Thursday night. No one went out on Thursday, not in my little gang anyway. But I had to see people. I rang Denise, Erin, even Charlotte, just to see if anyone would be up for coming round to listen to a few CDs, but everyone was busy doing what I knew *I* should be doing, i.e. schoolwork. Denise promised we'd go into town at the weekend.

I slumped into my room, as usual, on my own, just me and myself for company.

I hadn't done any painting since my bedroom escapade, so I got out my sketchpad and some pastels. I began to sketch faces, using my own face in my mirror as the model. Lots of different faces, all girls, with great hair and lovely eyes. Hair and eyes are things that can make you look very lovely.

Then I began to crayon the hair and eyes in all kinds of colours, until I had quite a fashion collection. I liked one that I'd done where the eyes were very dark with shadow, and a loose strand of hair swept across the forehead. It was a very sexy face, but deep and thoughtful. The dark eyes made you want to meet that girl and find out about her. Was she hiding behind her eye-shadow, or was she as up-front as the stereotype might have suggested?

I looked at myself in the mirror. And back at the sketch. I liked her more and more. She was beautiful.

I took a piece of board and began to mix up some acrylics, my favourite medium. I had given the girl in the sketch indigo-blue make-up, and I began to paint a new portrait using all the blues I could mix. I painted this wonderful girl in blue. I was up very late painting. Dad looked in on me about midnight I think, and I was still busy. He smiled, glanced at my sketches and said, 'It's nice to see you drawing again. You know you're very good.'

'Ta,' I said, and carried on with just a little smile back at him. I wanted to finish this girl before I slept.

I really liked her when she was done. I propped the board up on my desk and looked at her from across my room. She was so lovely, I could feel a little tear creep from my eye. She was someone I could really be close to. I whispered something to her, and she replied, 'Hiya. I'm Belle.'

nineteen

The next day was Friday and I didn't go to school. I told Mum I had bad period pains, and she phoned school. I went back to bed.

When I came round again it was nearly midday. I took a shower to try to open my eyes properly, but it didn't help much. I went back to my room and looked at my drawings again. I think I'm good at drawing. It frees my mind when I draw. I still draw a lot. That's one thing I've inherited from my dad that I'm pleased about. We've got paintings on our walls at home that he did, and that are excellent. He says he's always been frustrated because he really wanted to be an artist, not a graphic designer just doing commercial stuff. But if you saw his paintings, you'd be impressed. He did one of Mum, a portrait in watercolour, and she looks so beautiful in it. You can see how much he loves her by the way he painted her. He really does love her. And I know she gets on at him, but I also know she loves him and she loves that painting.

Anyway, I looked at my painting, the one I'd done the night before, and I decided to be as lovely as she was. I made myself look just like my image of the indigo girl. Deep eyeshadow, sharp black lashes. I sprayed my hair so it fell perfectly across my face, framing my left eye with a dramatic long curl. I used plenty of pale foundation so the blueness of my eyes was even more intense.

I became Belle.

The room had been a bit of a futile gesture. I guess I'd known from the start I'd have to suffer for that. But my face was mine and no one else's – Dad couldn't make me change that. He'd said I was very good at drawing, and he seemed to like those images I'd created. Good. So he'd like my new face. I was ready to start afresh. Belle would make me happy. So I thought.

twenty

I had a great week (Rollercoaster Effect again). I spent a couple of lunch-times doing homework for boys in return for cigarettes, and Denise and I smoked them in the store cupboard in the upper school art studio. When we'd finished, the cupboard was completely full of smoke, and I just wish I'd seen Mr Dawes open it the first time after lunch!

I began to think about hanging out with boys again. I'd noticed Peter Ferro looking at me all week. Peter's pretty desirable. Not very bright, but dead good-looking, with lovely dark hair and clear skin. I smiled at him a few times and I told him I thought his poem about football kits was funny. (He read it out in English Lit. – supposedly it was an attack on the exploitation of football fans by clubs who have loads of kits on the go at once. Was that really a suitable subject for literature? You have to feel sorry for boys really.)

George and Charlotte had split up, as Denise had predicted, and George had been sort of drifting around Denise and me. I began to semi-consider giving him another chance.

I was working well. I was staying up late, but I was buzzing. I could feel mathematical concepts slotting into place in my head. I began to think, 'Yeah, I can do this.' Perhaps, thinking about it now, I was staying up too late. I was creeping downstairs to make coffee at one and two in the morning, because I just couldn't stop once I got into the groove. I could see the A grades falling like confetti from the outstretched hands of ecstatic teachers.

Sometimes, late at night, I'd put on my dark eyeshadow and look at myself in the mirror and say, 'You are beautiful, Belle.' It seemed to give me strength, power.

I even wrote to dear Sam. It wasn't much of a letter, and compared to the bunch of unsent ones hidden at the bottom of my wardrobe, it said nothing. Just 'Hi, how are you, hope uni is going great, only a few weeks to my exams, I've finally chucked George' – that kind of thing, platitudes and white lies. The kind of thing we mostly say, all the time, to everyone. It was only me who wanted to say deep things. But anyway, I wasn't feeling deep, not that week.

As I said, I had a great week, and Denise and I went out at the weekend, done up to the nines. We went into town, couldn't get into the first place we tried, but the bouncer was gorgeous, so it was well worth a loud argument at the door. We went into a couple of trendy bistro bars, got chatted up in one of them, and walked home arm-in-arm, laughing and giggling. I was home by the eleven o'clock deadline so Dad and

Mum were pleased with me, and I fell upstairs and into bed feeling reborn.

Until Monday afternoon, in history. Then I felt dead and buried again.

twenty-one

My history teacher was never number one in my Top Humans Of All Time list. The fact that his nickname was Slob probably gives you a clue. But he was a good teacher, I suppose. He knew his stuff, could talk for whole lessons about historical events without reading his notes. So I guess I had a grudging respect for his knowledge.

The words, 'This is full of interesting opinion, but this is supposed to be a history essay, not creative writing. Please get your facts in place before giving your point of view', accompanied by the grade of C, did my head in. I sat in the classroom, and I can remember feeling warm sunshine lighting up my face and hair as I read through the essay, looking for something to argue with. He had written comments all over the essay as he always did, and each comment was so true. It didn't even deserve C – the essay was a load of BS. I'd been so enthusiastic about the topic that I'd gone off on a rambling tour of my mind and hadn't even given some key dates. How stupid of me! How ridiculous of me! How thick of me to think

I'd cracked it. A's and B's were illusions – C was reality.

But wait a minute – C is cool. C gets you your certificate. C gets you into the sixth form. C is a pass, at least at the moment. They might change it so A is a pass. But today, C is all you need. Unless you're me. Or, unless you're me as I was then. I could handle it now. And I think you should be happy with C, especially if trying to get A's is making your head go to mush. It's about knowing where you're comfortable and being content with that. But for me, then, C was a near-death experience.

I walked home after school in a daze. Denise was rabbiting away at me about our night out and how she was going to go back to the bar we'd been in where some guy had asked her out and blah blah blah. I wasn't listening: I was going over and over that damned essay in my mind, searching for a way out. But there was no way out. Dad had been laying off me since my grounding. I had begun to think we'd sorted ourselves out. But now I was shaking. How would he react if I told him my history grade had dropped to C?

'Are you listening?' Denise said.

'Oh sorry. I was thinking how I'm going to tell Dad I got a C for that history.'

'Don't tell him. Lie. Tell him you got an A.'

'He might want to read it.'

'Read it? You have got to be joking. No one reads history essays. Except Slob. Just tell him it was an A, and if he asks to read it tell him it's so brilliant it's had to be locked in the school vaults for the benefit of future generations.'

'I'm going to rewrite the whole essay and hand it in again, then I won't have to tell him at all because I'll get a better grade.'

'Hey! No! You mustn't do that. Listen, Belinda, I didn't want to say this before but this isn't normal. You're obsessing over this stupid essay. You do it all the time actually, but this is worse. It's one revision essay. And even if you do finish up with a C for history, it doesn't matter – you'll still get enough GCSEs to start your own school! You're a top student. Don't you know that?'

'But I don't want a C. I want an A.'

'But you can't guarantee it, even if you work from now till doomsday. Relax. You've done the work.'

'I can't relax. I can't stop worrying. I've worked so hard. I think about it all the time. I just can't stop.'

'I think you should talk to your mum or something. Maybe you should tell your dad – maybe he doesn't realise how frightened you are of what he'll say. I'm sure your dad wouldn't go mad. He's really nice. I like him. I actually fancy him a bit.'

'Denise!'

'Listen, tell your dad you got a C and he should be glad you got that given how hideous the teacher is.'

Denise was right about everything, and not just because of what she said, but because of how she said it. It all came out of her heart, out of love. That's the key to it.

She always said it doesn't matter if you get Z–, as long as you had a decent go. No one can say anything if you had a decent go. Maybe God gave you a brain that can't *ever* get more than Z– for history. Fine. So you'll just have to concentrate on your better subjects, like hanging out with your friends. You'll probably get A for that every time.

Denise was the only one I spoke to much. But she couldn't really know how I felt, because even I didn't really know. I just knew I couldn't tell Dad. I felt so low, so heavy that I could hardly speak. I wanted to tell Dad, because even if he did blast me out we would have sat down and worked through the essay together. But I'd got to the point where it wasn't just Dad I was worried about – I was frozen with misery. Don't let anyone say being depressed is all in the head, because that's not true. Your whole body feels it, your whole being. There's not a part of you that doesn't feel like it's encased in concrete. You can't move, you don't want to do anything, you feel useless, all your relationships seem worthless and meaningless. You are as near to being dead as you can be, except you're alive.

I concealed myself in my room again all evening, and I didn't mention the essay to Dad, or Mum. I just wanted to go to sleep, and maybe if I never woke up, that would be acceptable. I didn't want to die. I just didn't want to wake up, at least not until my exams were over.

You can no doubt see how irrational I was. But I couldn't see anything rationally because I was in my deep, dark hole.

If you are like me, and you suddenly find you can't enjoy anything, then you have to do something about it. Talk to your friends. If you haven't got friends, talk to your parents. If you haven't got parents, talk to your doctor. If you haven't got a doctor, talk to the postman. Don't bottle it up, because if you do, you'll end up like I was five chapters from here.

I cried myself to sleep, and when I woke in the middle of the night, still fully dressed, on top of my duvet, I was still crying. I'd been crying in my dreams. The room seemed so dark: my misery monster smothered every bit of light. I didn't know what to do. I was scared then, because I'd never felt that bad before. The weight of every single worry I'd ever had was pressing down on me, demanding a solution. But I could see no solutions at all.

Everything seemed hopeless, without a possibility of ever coming right.

twenty-two

I spent the last two weeks of term bright and witty at school, and silent at home.

I dragged myself along. I would wake up each morning feeling I could hardly breathe. It was such an effort to get dressed. I was eating, but I couldn't really taste the food. I didn't skive school again, though I had absolutely no interest in anything. I did no homework, no revision, nothing. I could have done some work on the history essay and resubmitted it. Mr Rogers didn't mind if you did that. But I couldn't be bothered. What was the point? I'd thought I'd been conquering my weaknesses, and I'd still got what for me was a fail grade.

I can quite easily see, especially when Louise and I are talking, how twisted my view of my life had become – pushing myself to breaking point wasn't exactly the best way to do well. But I couldn't see it like that then.

If Dad or Mum asked how things were going, I said, 'Fine.' I think I was almost banking on my GCSEs being rubbish so that my parents would finally realise I'd blown it. It would be a relief not to have to pretend to be high-flying Belinda any more. The obvious thing to do would have been to talk to them, but I didn't/couldn't.

Oddly, my end of term report promised an impressive set of GCSE results, and Dad and Mum were very pleased with it. Dad said I only had to put in a final sprint and I was home and dry. But what did the teachers or Dad really know? They only saw the outside, and I had stopped believing that I could succeed at anything.

I was convinced I was going to fail every subject, and I'd become so listless that I couldn't do a thing about it. I'd given up on everything. I was just drifting toward . . . whatever.

I would get home, do my hair and my make-up and look at myself in my mirror, dreaming of some alternative life as Belle. My life as Belinda seemed over.

No one knew how I was feeling. I could be bright enough in front of other people. I could join in the jollity at lunch-times and breaks at school, and at home it was easy to camouflage myself, because as long as I stayed in my room and appeared to be studying, Dad and Mum hardly saw me.

The only thing I had any time for was my paintings of Belle. My paintings of me. I must have done twenty or more new pictures, some sketched in pencil, some painted. I liked the glamour of losing myself in her.

On Saturday, the first day of the Easter holidays, Denise and I were supposed to be going into town to buy some clothes and meet up with our friends. But I didn't go. Instead, I caught the bus to another part of town, a part where there were junky antique shops, and shops that sold specialist things like aluminium car wheels and military paraphernalia. It was an old part of town, not at all 'high street'. None of the shops were the big names, and some were boarded up, or just half open. There were hand-written notices in some of the windows saying things like, 'If no one's here try the Coffee Bean', or 'Back in ten', or 'For sale, Victorian fireplace, ring Jon on 254336'. That kind of area.

I got off the bus and wandered up the main street and down a few side roads. I was looking for a place I'd seen advertised in the free paper. But I wasn't too sure of the road. Then I found what I was looking for, just a little sign on a door that opened into steep, narrow stairs.

I wasn't nervous. I walked up the stairs to a glass-panelled door decorated in colourful images of eagles and snakes and butterflies, with elaborate curly writing saying, 'Tristan Holyhead: Body Art'. I opened the door and looked into a world of magical transformation.

There was a young woman lying back on a leather padded chair. She was naked from the waist up, and one of her nipples was being pierced. The other one already had a silver ring through it. She smiled at me in a rather dazed way. The guy doing the work (Tristan, I assumed) didn't look up but carried on with his task. I sat on a plastic chair and watched, beginning to feel nervous, but fascinated still.

He was a big man, with long black hair tied back in a ponytail. He was wearing black jeans and a black cap-sleeved T-shirt. No piercings as far as I could see, and only the one tattoo, a beautiful little bluebird on his arm. He was really handsome too, by the way, just so you know.

He was very gentle with the woman, and when the ring was in place she smiled, then hugged him.

'What do you think?' he said as he dabbed her breasts with antiseptic spirit.

She stood up and admired herself in a tall mirror. She smiled and said, 'Fantastic.'

'They look lovely,' I said. And I meant it.

She put on a loose blouse and then a denim jacket. 'I'll pay you tonight,' she said to Tristan, kissing him on the cheek.

'No problem,' he said. He smiled at me then, and said, 'Hi. What can I do for you?'

'I want a nose stud.'

twenty-three

Tristan was very kind to me. He talked me through it, made sure I was certain I wanted the stud, and was so gentle I almost didn't feel the piercing until it was all over.

When it was done I stood up and stared into Tristan's mirror, completely amazed at myself. The deep sapphire blue of the stud was perfect for me. I was so excited. This was really me!

But I wasn't complete. I'd come with a purpose and there was another step to take, if I had the bottle. My heart was thumping.

No one else had come into the studio, and I needed to make a decision before Tristan had another customer. If I didn't do it quickly I knew I might not do it at all. Tristan obviously sensed I wasn't ready to leave – he looked at me (with gorgeous brown eyes!) and said, 'Are you OK? Is it what you expected?'

'Oh yes, it's great . . . but, there's something else . . . I want a tattoo as well,' I said.

'Are you sure? It's a lot more permanent than a stud – you can't take a tattoo off. Have you thought about this?'

'Yeah, I'm sure.'

'Do you know what you want?'

'A broken heart.'

'Broken? Should I ask who broke it?'

'I broke it myself,' I replied.

'Heavy,' Tristan said, almost mocking me. But when I didn't laugh, his tone of voice changed and he said, 'Have a look in the catalogues. If there's nothing there you like, I want you to do me a little drawing so I get it right. No one has ever asked me for a broken heart before. Can you draw?'

'Oh yes, I can draw,' I said, and I smiled at him. A connection was made, I'm sure of it. I haven't seen Tristan again, but I know we made a link that afternoon.

When I got home I went straight to my room and looked at myself in my long mirror, for several minutes, just admiring my new body. It was fantastic! I felt so strong and confident.

The lovely sapphire stud so suited me. And my heart was beautiful. Just below my hip, inside my pants, where no one would ever see it unless I wanted them to. It had just the slightest crack running through it, and Tristan said he could easily fill in the missing colour if my heart ever got mended. I adored it. It had hurt, but the pain made the achievement all the greater. I almost liked the pain.

I brushed my hair into my new style, dragging a lock of fair hair across my forehead. I made myself up again. I looked good.

A bit glamorous, a bit unconventional, a bit sexy. I liked myself.
I was high on being Belle.

I was still wearing my blue make-up when Dad came home from
work, halfway through the afternoon. He usually played golf on
Saturday, but he'd had to go into the office to finish an urgent
job. Mum was at a conference all day, and I had thought Dad and
I might have a little late lunch together. I'd made a pot of coffee,
ready for him, and cut some nice granary bread and mixed up a
salad. I'd done a little spread on the kitchen table.

'Did you get the job finished?' I said as he came into the
kitchen.

'Yeah, thank God,' he said. 'I might still sneak in a round of
golf if I get a move on.'

'Do you want some lunch?'

'Oh, yes please,' he said. Then, nodding his head in the
direction of my nose, 'What's that you've got?'

'A nose stud.'

'I hope it's not permanent.'

I tried to be humorous. 'What, my nose?'

He didn't laugh. 'The stud. You haven't had your nose
pierced, have you?'

'Yes. Do you like it?'

'Well . . . I'm not sure . . . I don't know if it suits you.'

'I think it does. The man who did it said I looked beautiful.'

'Oh, did he? Who is he? Is he competent to pierce people's

noses?' Dad said, already put out, I could tell.

'Yes. He's got a certificate.'

'It looks very sore. If nose studs go out of fashion, you're going to wish you hadn't had it done.' He started to move away, to go into the hall. I stood in front of him.

'Why can't you ever be nice to me? Why can't you say something nice to me instead of always telling me off?'

'I'm not telling you off, I'm just saying I'm a bit surprised. I'm just not sure it's you, that's all.'

'What *is* me?'

'Well, you know, you're more . . . middle of the road, a bit more . . . I don't know, intellectual?'

'Having a nose stud doesn't mean I've suddenly become a dunce.'

'It's an attitude though. I suppose it's normal. I suppose we all have our bit of rebellion. But you still have to fit in sooner or later. You can't opt out completely.'

'I'm not opting out! I just want a nose stud.'

'Well you've got one. If you're thinking of having any other bits of your body done, you ask me or Mum first.' He paused, and I thought that was going to be the end of it, but he was on Dredge Up Anything You Can Think Of mode by now, and said, 'By the way, you've been on the internet too much lately. It ties up the phone. You'll have to ease off on it.'

Now I was starting to get angry – we clashed like two pieces of flint. Sparks everywhere. 'Yes, Dad. Anything else I've done wrong? No? Good. Oh, I didn't tell you about my history essay, did I? Thought you might like to know, I got a C. I was very pleased actually because I did no work at all for it. That's how I intend to be from now on, so that next time you slag me off I'll be able to say, "You're right, Dad, I am a lazy good-for-nothing, and I deserve to fail all my exams because I wasted so much time having my nose pierced." '

'Have you finished?'

'I don't know.'

'We'll talk again when you've had a chance to think about what you've been saying.'

'You're the one who needs to think about what you've been saying.'

'Belinda! Watch yourself! Show some respect.'

'You don't show me any! You slag me off, you go on at me all the time to work harder, and even when I do work hard you don't notice. You never encourage me, you just nag.'

'That's not true! I do everything I can to encourage you. And if I do nag, it's because I'm trying to make sure you get what you want from life.'

'Do you know what I really want? Do you?'

'. . .'

'No, you don't! What I really want is a father who cares about *me*, not about my grades, or if my image is suitable. You only want me to do well at school so you can boast to your friends about me. I don't care if I fail every exam! I want to be a hippie in a commune, with people who really know how to live! I'm fed up with doing what *you* want. I hate it!' I know I was being vile to him, but I couldn't stop myself.

I remember that moment so well. He stood there, in the middle of the kitchen, holding his jacket in one hand, his portfolio case in the other. He looked at me with tired eyes, and for a second I thought he was going to say something else, but he just walked past me. I heard him go up the stairs.

I still find it hard to think about that moment.

I don't hate my dad. I love him. He only wanted the best for me, urging me to succeed, guiding me in the right way to behave. It had worked with Sam. Sam had responded with a grin and a swagger and had lurched through all his exams and gone off on his university adventure. Sam knew how to play by the rules and still have his fun. Whereas I had got drunk and come home late, trashed my room, skived school, and had my nose pierced (and got a tattoo I didn't dare tell him about, and still haven't). I'd let him down. *I'd* messed up again. If I hated anyone, it was me.

Depression is dangerous. It tricks you into feeling bad about everything, even normal things. Arguments with parents are normal. Parents know that, kids know that. *I* know that, now. But after Dad walked away from me I felt like I'd been cut into pieces. I sat at the kitchen table and didn't cry. I just stared at nothing, as still as stone.

Dad came back down and ate some lunch, while I sat there in silence. He smiled when he'd finished, and said, 'Listen, I'm sorry I shouted. The nose stud's not my cup of tea, but if you want it, it's fine. Thanks for doing lunch. I'm going to the club. See you later.' Then he kissed me on the cheek and left. To him, I suppose nothing much had happened — just another family tug-of-war. But I was wiped out. I wandered up to my room, flopped on to my bed and fell asleep.

I woke up when Mum came home. She called a cheery hello and I returned the greeting, but I stayed put. A bit later Dad came back, and I could hear them talking downstairs. About me, I supposed. I was expecting one of them to come up and reopen the nose stud debate, but they left me alone. I think sometimes I used to want the confrontation, just so things would be said. But this time they let me be, and I was on my own with my brooding. How I wish I had told them everything.

I spent the early evening in my room, gazing at my tattoo and my nose stud, my new identity.

Then I decided to go out.

twenty-four

I showered and washed my hair, did my make-up and put on a short going-out dress and the same shoes I had borrowed from Mum for Erin's party. I didn't ask her. She was in the lounge with Dad as I left. I shouted, 'I'm out with Denise. Back later.'

'Where are you going?'

'Probably into town. I'm going to Denise's first and we'll decide.'

'Don't be late. Back by eleven,' Mum said.

'Phone if you want me to pick you up,' Dad called.

'OK,' I replied. I neglected to mention I'd taken my mobile phone out of my handbag and left it in my dressing-table drawer. 'Bye.'

I caught the bus into town. I got out at the bus station and found a passport photo booth. I wanted a picture of myself. I still look at that strip of photos sometimes and wonder who that girl was. I headed for the bar where Denise and I had been chatted up. I wasn't going to make a fool of myself, I was just going to test my new me. The bouncer on the door didn't really pay me much attention as I walked past him. I knew I looked too young, but he didn't seem to care. It all depends on their mood. He just smiled at me and I breezed in. The bar was pretty full and I suddenly felt nervous. But I wasn't backing out.

It was a really swish place, like some retro furniture store, all chrome and glass, and very bright, with too-loud music pumping your blood pressure up. As I walked in, I felt my heartbeat lift. I loved the look of the people in there – fashionable and young and independent. I had become one of them.

I walked to the bar and ordered a sensible drink. I didn't want to get drunk; I wanted to enjoy every minute of my adventure. I'd be home by eleven, easily. I just wanted to prove myself.

I stayed at the bar and one of the barmen started talking to me. He was too old to be interesting, but each time he passed on his way to pour another drink he smiled. He asked if I was alone. I said I was waiting for a friend and if she didn't hurry up I was going on without her. I began to believe my story myself.

'Where are you going then?' the barman asked.

'Oh, Fantasy, probably. There's a few of us who meet up there. Or I might go home if I get bored.' I was cool. I was offhandedly vague, as if I really didn't care what happened that night.

A group of lads came into the pub and headed for the bar in a noisy scrum of energy. I recognised one of them from the time before, and my stomach flipped. I turned away from them and concentrated on my drink, which had suddenly become very demanding of attention. I didn't know whether to let this guy see me, or hide and get out. I wanted to be chatted up again, but without Denise to do the loud banter I wasn't sure I could handle it. But that's why I'd come. In my dress and shoes, and nose stud and tattoo.

So I turned round and faced the room. I watched the boy-man and his friends as they talked and laughed. Some girls had joined up with the little huddle and it looked like they were having a great time. Denise and I could have a great laugh, but this was different. This was better because it had nothing to do with my usual life. That was the attraction. I wanted to be out of my life. I didn't want to die – I just wanted a different life where I could start again and be me without any pressure from people (including myself) who had expectations.

I was running away. But you can't run from yourself. When you run away from yourself all you do is wear out your shoes.

I began to concentrate on the boy. He was handsome, quite small, with cropped fair hair. I think he was about eighteen or nineteen – I'm not sure – but I liked the fact that he was older than me. I wanted to catch his eye, and I was sure that if I looked at him hard enough he'd sense me.

The boy saw me. I smiled straight back at him. Then I carried on looking at him, even when he turned back to his friends, and when he looked my way again, our eyes met again. This time he twigged. I could see the recognition on his face. He came over to me.

'Hi. On your own?' he said.

'Yeah. I've been stood up by my girlfriend.'

'Oh, who's that? That one you were with before?'

'Yes. I think her dad must have caught her. He's really strict and he makes her stay in if he thinks she's pubbing. We're under-age.'

'You don't look it,' he said. 'What's your name?'

'Belle.'

'Hi, Belle. I'm Lee.'

'Hi.'

'So, do you want to join us? Until your girlfriend arrives?'

'Yeah, thanks. Will your friends mind?'

'No! They'll be glad to meet you. Actually, we're going to a party later. You can come if you want.'

'Great!'

I spent the evening with Lee's crowd. They seemed to accept me as if I'd always known them. Lee gave me a lot of attention, and I lost myself in the noise and smoke, and a lovely floating feeling of being in a glossy TV drama, in which this was my first episode. Before I knew it, it was half-past eleven and we were walking along the road, in the midst of others on their way to clubs and wine bars. I knew I'd missed the last bus home. I knew I was already late. I suppose I knew that Dad and Mum would already be worried and angry because I wasn't back and hadn't phoned. But I didn't care. At that moment I didn't care about anything in my life, except being with Lee.

'So, are you up for this party?' he said.

'Where is it?'

'Over near the football ground. Joe's gonna drive – he hasn't been drinking.'

I have a memory of thinking, I shouldn't do this. I've had my fun. I'm only sixteen. Go home. But I also remember thinking, What is there to go home for? I'll get ripped into for being late, and taking Mum's shoes, and I'll have to lie about where I've been.

I didn't want to go home, at least I thought I didn't. So I threw my arm round Lee's neck and said, 'Yeah! I'm up for it!'

twenty-five

I was feeling exhilarated as we piled into Joe's car and we
zoomed off, with music throbbing out of huge speakers in the
back. I was thinking, Wow! This is fun.

But, as the car bounced along the road, I began to feel a bit
sick. On the back seat, with Lee and two of his friends squashed
in beside me, the movement of the car and the pounding, pulsing
music was making my head spin. I stopped feeling floaty and
groovy and started feeling ridiculous. That come-down again.
But so soon. I'd thought I was on a good safe high this time, with
everything sorted – my stud, my hair, my make-up, my tattoo,
my identity. But I suddenly found I was still Belinda inside all that
magical transformation, and I'd turned back into the scrambled
egg of a girl I really was. I felt like I'd been abducted by aliens,
except I'd volunteered to be abducted.

We arrived at the party house. I'd never been to the football,
and it wasn't a part of town I knew. It was a dark street of small
terraced houses with cars parked all along the road. It was a

warmish evening and a few people were outside, sitting on the front wall and standing in the doorway. I recognised some others from the bar.

I followed Lee into the house and into a dimly lit room where people were talking loudly and laughing. There was very loud music crashing out from another room and, for a second, I felt a little dizzy again. Lee seemed to dissolve into the hubbub of people, and I was left standing in the middle of the crush, surrounded by faces I'd never seen before in my life. I tried to mingle but I couldn't think of a thing to say to anyone. Being a flirt at Erin's party had been easy; this was not at all the same sketch.

I spotted the barman who'd spoken to me earlier – I tried to quickly turn away, but he'd seen me and pushed his way through the tangle of bodies, until he was right up inside my personal bubble. 'Hello again!' he said. 'Did your friend ever turn up?'

'Uh, not exactly. I'm with Lee,' I said, hoping that would put him off.

'Lee! Oh dear! Sharon won't be very happy!' he said, laughing.

'Who's Sharon?'

'Lee's girlfriend.'

'Is she here?' I said.

'Of course, it's her house!'

My heart collapsed. I felt my face flush. I suddenly knew I'd made a big mistake, and I knew I was somewhere I really shouldn't be. 'Well, I'm not with him like *that*,' I said, desperately trying to sound as if I knew what the hell was going on. 'I just came with him, in Joe's car.' That gave the barman the green light.

'So, you're on your own?'

'Well, my friend should be here soon.'

'Well, let me get you a drink.'

'No ta. I'm feeling a bit carsick. Joe drove a bit fast.'

'Come on, you'll be all right. I'll get you something!' He went off, but quickly came back with a drink that smelt and tasted very alcoholic. I sipped at it but it was too strong. I put the glass on a coffee table and tried to retreat into a corner away from the pressure of people. The barman stayed close. I was starting to feel scared now.

'How about a dance?' he said.

'In here?' I said. There was hardly room to move, let alone dance.

'In the back room. Come on!' He took my hand and pulled me out into the hall and into another room where the hi-fi was. The music was so loud my eardrums shuddered in protest, but the barman wanted to dance, and I seemed unable to do anything else. So we shuffled around to some poppy dance nonsense.

I saw Lee pass by the door with a blonde draped across him – Sharon, I assumed. I was annoyed. Lee had kind of led me on. Or maybe I'd led myself on. He hadn't said anything to me about a Sharon, but then why should he?

I was dancing automatically, half aware of my barman jigging away aimlessly. What on earth was I doing? Was this fun?

Wouldn't it have been more fun at the bowling alley with Denise and the gang? A few rounds of bowling, a takeaway kebab, and perhaps a little trial snog with Peter on the bus home. That would have been all right, really.

Then I thought of Dad and the absolute nuclear war I was in for when I finally got home. I thought of my mother and wondered where she was tonight. Always in the back of my mind – my low-life mother, bugging me from the bottom of her pond.

I was snapped out of my wanderings by the barman grabbing me and pulling me up to him. 'By the way, my name's Merv!' he yelled, trying to get above the music.

'Right,' I replied. He was moving too close to me, trying to be sexy. I didn't like him at all. I tried to pull back a bit, but he kind of stuck to me. I felt his hand move to my behind, and I dearly wished I'd worn jeans instead of a clingy dress.

'I've got to go to the loo,' I said.

I pulled away and nearly ran to the hallway and up the stairs. There was a queue for the toilet, but I waited there. The girl in front of me in the queue was trying to get a snog off the man ahead of her. She was kind of hanging from his shoulders, obviously the worse for drink, trying to manoeuvre herself into a kissing position. I found myself thinking, Slapper.

The man wasn't interested, but she kept on until he pushed her away with a curse. Wobbling on her high heels, she swayed backwards and into me. She turned, smiling apologetically, her eyes senseless. Then she suddenly lost control of her feet, tried to regain her balance and dropped her wine glass. It smashed on the floor and red wine and shards of glass fired out across the bare floorboards. She began to giggle uncontrollably, and just stepped over the mess as the queue moved along.

I felt I could be sick. Who *were* these people? I felt tired. Very tired. I needed to get away, find somewhere to rest.

I left the queue and tried a door to a bedroom. As I began to open it I heard a woman laughing in the room, a man's voice slammed out, 'F*** off!' and I shut the door very quickly. The girl in the queue thought it was very funny and was consumed again, but I was aghast.

I was shaking now. I tried another door, and went into the room. It was dark, but the curtains were open and there was enough light to see a double bed, and I just fell on to it. I curled myself up into a tight little ball and tried to hide. In the dark and relative quiet of the room, I could hear my thoughts again. I'd been stupid. I'd wanted to go out on a limb; I'd wanted to be big and confident and in charge. But this wasn't any good. This wasn't my world; these people weren't anything to do with me. They were all loud-mouthed, incapable drunks.

And what was I? A serious person who wanted to go somewhere in life, an individual who knew what she wanted, a young adult making her own decisions? I wasn't any of these things. I was a flop, a failure, an abandoned child, a truant, a C student trying to make an A. I'd crashed out of the race at the first hurdle. I couldn't handle my own life, so I'd tried to invent a new one. And now I was in it I hated it just as much as the one I was running from. It wasn't anyone's fault but mine. Whatever I did, whatever I tried, I would come down to this feeling. I was in my hole again. But instead of being in my hole in my warm, safe home, with parents I could safely rebel against, I was in my hole in an unfamiliar part of town with a houseful of strangers.

I felt so miserable. I lay there, quietly allowing my unhappiness to run out of my eyes, while all around me people were deliriously happy in their party. This was how it always was, really. Me in a black hole: the rest of the world out there enjoying life.

In a dark room, in the home of a person I'd never met, I was at my lowest, weakest point, and I truly didn't have a clue what to do next. I felt that my life couldn't get any worse.

And then the door opened and in danced Merv the barman.

twenty-six

'Ah! There you are!' Merv said. The sound of the party slammed in for a second, and then Merv closed the door.

I shivered, and didn't answer. I knew I was in trouble. I lay still, hoping he'd go away if I said nothing. Maybe he'd think I was asleep.

'Is this your way of saying you love me?' Merv said.

Oh God, I felt scared. I didn't want to speak. I just wanted to stay still and pretend the outside world wasn't there. But I was still in touch enough to know I had to do something to get out of this. 'I'm not feeling well . . . my head's dizzy,' I said. I didn't look, but I heard his heavy footfall as he came towards me.

'You've had a bit too much to drink, that's all,' he said. 'Sit up and you won't feel so dizzy.' He came over and lifted me out of my curled-up hiding position, until I was sitting upright on the bed. He sat, behind me, his arms right round my shoulders and across my chest. His face was so close to mine that I could smell his pungent breath. 'How d'you feel now?'

'Uhh, not so good,' I said, never looking at him. In the dark at least I could pretend I had some privacy, and if I didn't make eye contact perhaps he'd get the hint and go away.

'I'll make you feel better,' he said, and he planted a kiss on my cheek.

I really didn't know what I should do. I was suddenly so young, so inexperienced, so naive, and I didn't want to be in this room with this man, but I didn't know how to get away. But there was also something very odd about the way I felt. I didn't like Merv, but I was excited by the situation. I knew the situation was bad, but I also knew I didn't want to go home. I knew I couldn't handle what was happening to me, but I wanted to see it through. I'd come this far down the road – I might as well get to the next corner before I decided whether to turn back.

I turned my head to face him. He wasn't handsome, not very young, and I didn't fancy him in the slightest. When I think back to that moment it is right up in my Top Ten Of All-Time Dumb Things To Do. But I did it. I kissed him. On the lips. And he responded in the way I'd so often fantasised about. He was enthusiastic, sure of himself. For a moment I had what I wanted. For a minuscule moment I enjoyed it.

Then I felt a touch on my knee. And then that touch became a hand moving up my leg, towards the hem of my dress. I dared to imagine for a split heartbeat that it was a nice touch, a touch that I would like. But Merv's hand kept moving along my leg. It slid along my thigh and inside my dress. It was like an electric shock to my brain and I snapped up to my feet. 'No!' I shouted.

'Hey! What's the matter?' Merv said.

'Don't do that,' I said. 'Don't *do* that!'

'I'm sorry, I thought you were up for it.'

'Well, I'm not.'

'It's not nice to tease,' he said in an angry tone.

'I'm sorry . . . I'm not feeling well, I told you.' I was so messed up, I began to cry.

'OK, it's all right, come here,' Merv said, pulling me back and holding on to me again. He began to stroke my hair and wipe the tears away from my eyes. He began to kiss me again, and suddenly I was fighting for survival. His hands were everywhere at once, his arms held me tight, his mouth was all over mine, I couldn't breathe, and I was shouting, 'Leave me alone! Get off me! Get off!'

The door flew open, the light came on and two blokes were yelling at us. I don't know what they were saying because I was screaming mindlessly, hitting out at Merv and running away, down the stairs and barging my way out into the street. I walked off in an outpouring of tears. There were voices behind me, I remember that, and I turned to see Merv and the other blokes coming along the pavement after me. They were shouting at me and I started running as fast as I could, in a blind panic. I don't know if they were chasing me, or just wanted to make sure I was all right. In my high heels I nearly stumbled, so I pulled them off and ran on barefoot. I didn't stop running until I found myself at a main road. I stopped for a second and then ran straight across. I ran along a side road, and down an alley. I had no idea where I was. The alley was narrow, between two houses, and I came out into a huge, dark, open space. Playing fields ahead, trees all around, with a path running across the park. My heart was still pumping crazily. I carried on running, right across the football pitches, right into the black centre of the field, until I simply couldn't run any more. I stopped. I stood still for a second, trying to catch my breath, and then I was suddenly violently sick. I felt so ill I couldn't stop myself. My stomach muscles felt like they'd been ripped out of me.

Eventually the retching stopped, and I sat down on the damp grass, in the darkness, in the middle of the playing field.

I was strangely calm, just sitting there in the dark. No one was coming. I was safe. I liked the black space and the silence. I sat for a while, breathing easier, not really thinking of anything, just allowing my mind to hover in the darkness. As my eyes began to adjust I could see patches of stars in the half-cloudy sky. It was soothing to be there.

My stomach churned, and for a moment I thought I might be sick again, so I got up and walked on until I came to another path. I walked out of the park into a badly lit street of semi-detached houses. I didn't know where I was going; I was just walking, on auto-pilot, mindlessly, until I finally hit a road I recognised. I was two or three miles from home, but I seemed not to care. I could have found a call box and phoned Dad, but I didn't want to. I liked being adrift.

* * *

It was half-past two in the morning when I reached Denise's house. I don't think I'd consciously gone there, but perhaps she was the only one I believed I could turn to now.

I stood beneath Denise's window and tried to think. I picked up a handful of gravel from a flowerbed and threw it upwards. Some must have hit her window because her light came on and her curtains rippled. She peered out, and I stared up at her. And then I passed out.

twenty-seven

Denise was as lovely as I could have imagined she would be.

I was lucky. I fell across a shrub, and she said I kind of crumpled rather than fell, so I didn't bash my head when I went down. I remember coming round in her arms, still on her front path.

'Oooh, sorry,' I said, as if I'd just trodden on her toe or something. 'I'm all right.' And I tried to stand up, promptly flopped back into her arms and nearly sparked out again.

'Come on, you're coming inside,' she said, like a teacher to a naughty pupil. She walked me inside, and put me in a big chunky armchair with about thirty cushions.

I sat there in a ball, hugging my legs, crying, for what seemed like hours. She kneeled in front of me, stroked my knee and tried to get me to stop crying. She smoothed my hair and told me everything was all right, until my sobbing eventually faded. I was in a kind of trance, and it was a long time before I could speak or even properly react to where I was or what Denise was saying.

I remember looking into her eyes and crying again, but crying because I was happy, happy because I was with someone I loved. It was such a relief to be back in my real life again.

Denise's mum had come down to see what was going on, and she made me a cup of hot chocolate, frothy and really sweet, and gave me a baggy sweatshirt to put on because I was shivering.

'What on earth has happened?' she asked. God knows what I must have looked like. My make-up must have been like a Dracula impersonation by then.

I found it hard to speak at all, and I could only manage small words and short phrases. I had this strange sensation, as if I was trapped inside my own head and only fragments of me could make it to the outside world. It took me a long time to get it all out, but I told them as much as I could make sense of.

'Did this Merv hurt you?' Denise asked, when I'd come to some kind of conclusion.

'No.'

'Do you want me to call the police?' Denise's mum said.

'Oh no. It was my fault!' I began to well up again.

'OK, you're OK,' Denise said, throwing her arms round me.

'I was scared . . . I thought he was going to . . . but nothing happened.'

'It's all right, we understand.'

'Can I stay here tonight?' I said.

'No,' Denise's mum said, 'you must go home. Your parents will be worried sick.'

'I don't want to go home.'

'Why? What's wrong?'

I cried again, in hurting, salty waves that gave me a headache. Everything I thought of made me so sad I couldn't stop the tears. I had never cried as much. It was as if all the bad days I'd been storing were overflowing out of my misery hole, in a huge tidal wave of darkness. It felt awful, but it was the best thing that could have happened. I needed all this to come out into the light.

I told them everything. I told them how I couldn't stop thinking about my mother, how I always felt like a failure no matter how hard I tried, how I always let my dad down, how I hated myself so much I wished I could be anyone but me, how I wished I could die so there'd be no more rubbish to deal with. I showed them my stud, and my tattoo, still red and sore.

When I'd finished, they were both holding me tight, and Denise was wiping the tears from my eyes with a tissue, and saying, 'You are my best-ever friend. You're the best person I know. You shouldn't talk like that. You're brilliant. You're lovely.' She was just smothering me in nice words.

'Belinda, you must talk to your parents – this is serious,' Denise's mum said. I remember how calm and clear her voice was. 'The way you're feeling is not healthy – you need help with this. I'm going to phone your parents and tell them you're safe, then I'm going to take you home, and you must tell them what's been going on. You must talk to them.' She was right. That was the best advice anyone ever gave me.

We stood at my front door, and I told Denise and her mum I wasn't going in, so Denise rang the bell. There I was in Denise's sweatshirt, with her arm round me, with my nose stud and my runny make-up, and my slinky dress and high heels, feeling like a helpless baby. Dad came to the door in his dressing-gown, looking semi-dazed. Mum stood next to him, and even in my deranged condition I could see the tears standing in her eyes. I threw myself into Mum's arms.

Mum was amazing. She did everything she could for me – she told her boss she had to take unpaid leave from work to be with me. And she stayed with me for a week while the doctor helped me settle down. The doctor said I needed rest and peace, and time to recover. He gave me some tablets, at first, to stabilise my emotions, and made arrangements for me to see Louise because he said the counselling would be really important. Mum stuck to me like glue until she knew I was coping. For days, she kept saying over and over that it was her fault: 'I *knew* you weren't well,' she kept saying. Of course, it wasn't her fault, but I will always love her for wanting to take the blame away from me. That was so, so kind of her.

Sam came home for his Easter break and treated me like a delicate flower. All I could do was sit around and read or watch TV. I was very shaky for quite a few days, and I cried a lot. I found it hard to see people, and I couldn't always say much. And

Sam, love the big lump, really looked after me while he was home. He even went as far as cooking me bacon and eggs for breakfast in bed one morning – he claimed it took all his courage to conquer his fear of the kitchen.

I'll never be like Sam. He's like a piece of tough rubber. I'm made of eggshell. I have to be careful with myself. But now I understand that, I think I can enjoy Sam's thick-necked way with everything, and I don't have to beat myself up because I'm not a female version of him.

Dad was great. Over the weeks that followed, I know he found it as hard as I did to talk, but we hugged often, and he really came through for me. He was practical and efficient, and he never made a fuss. He went into school and sorted it out so I could stay at home until my exams began. He helped me with my revision, and kept telling me it didn't matter what happened in the exams as long as I was all right. He even said I didn't have to sit the exams at all if I didn't want to: he said I could leave school and go to the FE college next year.

But I wanted to see the year through. I was still me, despite all my efforts to dismantle myself, and one thing I like about me is that I don't quit – I was going to do those damn exams, and if I got ten Z's, fine. All the teachers were really kind and they sent me work I could do at home. Denise was fantastic – so loving towards me, so generous with her loopy, bubbly love. She came round almost every evening with gossip and news and we revised a lot together. It was good medicine.

It's difficult now to believe that it all happened as I've described it, but I know it did – I can *feel* it. I can still get the heebie-jeebies when I think about some of the stuff I went through.

I know I'm not cured – Louise has explained this – you have to learn to live with the fact that you could get depressed again, anytime, maybe throughout your whole life. You'll still get days when you might feel sad, but you can get a balance. You can talk about the things that upset you, and you can admit to your family and your best friends that you aren't coping. You can let them know how you really feel, and you can remind yourself that you have things in your life to be happy about. You don't have to hide yourself behind studying obsessively, or by isolating yourself, or by crazy behaviour. At the end of the day, you have to be true to yourself, and that might mean accepting you need help. I needed help, very badly. I should have asked for help, like I would have with any other kind of problem. I could have asked Dad or Mum, or Denise, but I tried to fight my misery monster alone, until I couldn't fight any more, and I broke into pieces.

I've been put back together by love and kindness, I guess. Louise gets me to talk about absolutely anything that's on my mind, and she helped me and Dad and Mum to talk to each other. I still find it hard sometimes – but it's a lot easier to deal with the bad days now I know they understand me better, and I can go to them when I'm in trouble.

My GCSE results will be out soon. I can't help worrying, but whatever happens I know I did my best. And I know I can't be top of the class at everything. After all, nobody's perfect.

THE BEGINNING

appendix

If you have any anxiety about depression do talk to your friends, parents, teachers or doctor. For information on depression, you could also contact the following:

Fellowship of Depressives Anonymous
Box FDA
c/o Self Help Nottingham
Ormiston House
32–36 Pelham Street
Nottingham
NG1 2EG
Tel: 01702 433 838
(A support organisation for depressives)

Information Service
Royal College of Psychiatrists
17 Belgrave Square
London
SW1X 8PG
Tel: 020 7235 2351 extn: 138 or 152
Website: www.rcpsych.ac.uk/info
(For fact sheets and leaflets on mental health issues)

MIND

Granta House

15/19 Broadway

London E15

Tel: 020 8519 2122

(The mental health charity. Publishes literature on a range of mental health issues)

Useful phone lines

Childline	0800 1111
Samaritans	08457 90 90 90

Useful websites

www.childline.org.uk

www.depressionalliance.org.uk

www.mind.org.uk

(Contains downloadable information)

www.nhs.uk/depression

(The National Health Service online library)

www.samaritans.org.uk

Your doctor's surgery or health centre will also have leaflets.

Georgie's life is falling apart. Her mum is in a psychiatric hospital and her dad just isn't coping. No one has any idea what's going on in Georgie's head. And what's going on inside Georgie's head worries her. A lot. Her teachers say she isn't trying hard enough and her friends say she is dead weird. Georgie is pretty sure she's slowly going mad like her mum.

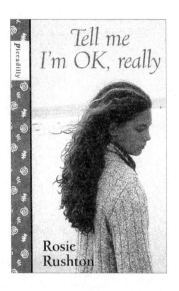

Then, just when she thinks she has lost it, Georgie meets Flavia Mott, a woman who at first seems even dottier than Georgie's mum. And suddenly Georgie finds herself opening up for the first time in years. But is it already too late for Georgie? Will she ever be OK again?

From the highly acclaimed author of:
The Leehampton Quartet
The Girls series
The Best Friends trilogy

If you would like more information about
books available from Piccadilly Press and
how to order them, please contact us at:

Piccadilly Press Ltd.
5 Castle Road
London
NW1 8PR

Tel: 020 7267 4492
Fax: 020 7267 4493

Feel free to visit our website at
www.piccadillypress.co.uk